Acknowledgements

Once again we'd like to thank our teen readers
Cecilia Ohanian and Kristen Hill.

A special thanks to our editor, Chris Boutee,
for her magic red pencil, and Liz Wong for
her spot-on illustrations.

Thanks to our families for
their continuous support and to our readers.

D0027211

A few fun facts about Kilimanjaro

Kilimanjaro, or the Roof of Africa as it is called, stands 19,366 feet high. That is the equivalent of 64.45 stacked football fields!

Climbing the mountain is more like a very steep walk with little oxygen; you don't need ropes and clamps.

Everyone from ten-year-olds (the minimum legal climbing age) to old people like your parents can reach the summit.

Part of what makes climbing Kilimanjaro unique is that the mountain creates its own weather. Plus you can pass through four different habitats in just days—from rainforests with monkeys chattering in the trees to heath and moorland filled with giant lobelia you would never find in your own backyard. The climb continues into an alpine desert with giant groundsels looming over you that look like they belong in a Dr. Seuss book. The desert leads to the Ice Cap where almost nothing lives, and blinding snowstorms occur without warning. Approaching the summit in the early morning hours, you feel for a moment as if you could reach out and touch the stars, because you are now among them.

SpyGirls Press
P.O. Box 1537
Fairfax, VA 22038
Visit our website at www.spygirlspress.com

First Edition: October 2016

The characters and events portrayed in this book are fictitious.
Any similarity to real persons, living or dead, is coincidental
and not intended by the authors.

Library of Congress Cataloging-in-Publication Data
Mahle, Melissa and Dennis, Kathryn
Camp Secret/Melissa Mahle and Kathryn Dennis
Illustrations by Liz Wong

1st ed. P. cm. – (Junior Spies Series, Book 2)
Summary: From the basement of the White House to
the snows of Kilimanjaro, the Junior Spies race against time
in their first mission to save the president of the United States.

ISBN – 978-0-9979545-0-0
[1. Action & Adventure – Fiction.
2. Mysteries & Detective – Fiction.]
Library of Congress Control Number: 2016913544

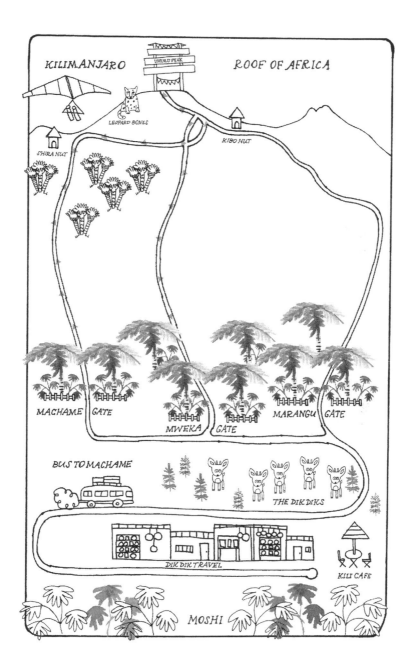

OPERATION UNDERCOVER

By

Melissa Mahle & Kathryn Dennis

This material has been reviewed
by the CIA to prevent the disclosure
of classified information.
(really)

Contents

① Flash

Day 1. 11:00 am, San Francisco, California

Kilimanjaro, Tanzania

At 10,000 feet the headaches start. Low, throbbing ones that make you want to lose your lunch. At 15,000 feet, the headaches become constant, but you don't notice any more. It takes all your concentration just to fill your lungs and keep your feet moving. At 19,710 feet, each step becomes a monumental effort. You move in slow motion, like you are an astronaut walking on the moon. You angle your hiking pole in the loose stones underfoot, take a step and gasp for air. This is the danger zone. Moving too fast could cause your brain to fill with fluid and swell, killing you slowly with each painful breath.

Audrey put down her book, unable to concentrate on the reading for her English Honors class. The words blurred across the page as her mind wandered. The clock at the front of the room ticked loudly; the timed assignment would end soon. Each tick made Audrey think about the beating of her heart when she was doing something important and exciting. Instead, she was sitting in a classroom at Sacred Heart Middle School in San Francisco, far away from anything exciting. Not like camp.

The last two months at summer camp had changed her life forever. Not that she could talk about it with any of her friends. She was sworn to secrecy, for life. Even if she did tell, who would believe a thirteen-year-old girl they called Aud-ball behind her back?

Audrey's sports watch began to vibrate. She hid her hand in the folds of her skirt, while casting a glance toward Sister Maria Teresa. The nun was prowling about, wooden ruler cocked, ready to fire at daydreaming girls. Selecting the mode button and then tapping the stopwatch toggle three times in rapid succession, Audrey sneaked a look at the LCD display, which had switched from a watch face to a data screen.

! FLASH. LOOK OUT WINDOW. COW-BOY!

Audrey looked up and gasped. A sandy-haired boy in a leather jacket and jeans waved at her from the other side of the glass. He wore a big goofy grin just like the last time she saw him. He had the biggest heart that he tried to hide under a rough cowboy act, but Audrey could see right through that. She could see…see…OMG.

Springing from her chair, Audrey rushed to the front of the room. She had to divert attention away from the window.

She leapt high and long, a practiced move from years of ballet. As her right shoe made contact with the polished wood, she started an uncontrolled slide, stopping just short of Sister Maria Teresa. A chorus of girls snickered behind her.

"I need to go to the bathroom, Audrey whispered, pushing her red hair back into a ponytail.

Her English teacher, whose face was permanently etched in a frown, said, "Cross your legs. Class is over in ten minutes."

"It's an emergency."

The ruler in Sister Maria Teresa's hand snapped to attention, causing the eighth grade class to freeze.

"Pleeeese," Audrey pleaded.

The nun looked over her black-framed reading glasses. Audrey held her breath. She always followed the rules, respected her teachers, and tried to get along with her classmates. *Make an exception for me*, Audrey silently screamed.

"Don't make it a habit," the Sister snapped.

Audrey shot out into the hall. Instead of turning right to the bathrooms, she turned left to the doors leading to the quad. She grabbed Tex and pulled him away from the window into the bushes below.

"What are you doing here? Trying to get me expelled? This is an all-girls school!"

"So you can't be seen in public with a guy, but you can be caught in the bushes with one?"

Audrey burst out laughing as she gave Tex a hug. She pretended not to notice his sudden awkward stiffness and asked the question she was sure he was waiting for.

"Why are you here and not in Texas?"

"The team's being activated. CONTROL wants us at Intel Center Headquarters, pronto."

Audrey beamed. She would see her friends again. They all lived in different states. Ria Santos, agent PUZZLE-GIRL, lived in Virginia, and Lee Wong, agent LAB-MAN, was in New York. "What's the mission?"

"Dunno. I just got a message with contact instructions. You know CONTROL; she's always short on details until she decides to give you the full briefing."

Even after spending the better part of a summer under her direction, CONTROL was still a wonderful mystery to Audrey. But Tex was not. "So you decided to hop a plane and deliver the news personally to me?" Audrey said, looking deep into Tex's eyes.

"Ah, not quite." Tex pulled a leaf off the bush, pretending to be very interested in it. "I happened to be in the area and decided to howdy you in person."

"In the area?"

"Yeah."

"Yeah, why?" Audrey nudged Tex to get him to look at her again. She needed to feel what was going on inside her friend. Ever since she was little, she had a special knack of sensing other people's thoughts and feelings.

"I've been down in LA sprint car racing. Those dudes are totally laid back and don't bother me about being only thirteen." His grin sprang back. Tex loved racing anything and everything.

"Not in school?"

The grin slipped away. "Naw. Expelled, for acting out too many times."

"Ah, Tex, you're too smart for that. Do you think CONTROL's going to keep you on the team if you don't graduate? Think about the team. We need you."

"It's easy for you, MIND-READER; you're as smart as a hooty owl."

Tex looked dejected, crouched against the concrete, eyes cast down. Even though her first instinct was to hug him, she knew what he really needed was some help. "Sounds like you just need to find a school that's a better fit for you, COWBOY."

"Is there room here? I'd look good in a skirt." Tex asked, playfully tugging on her regulation red and navy plaid uniform skirt.

Audrey giggled, despite her effort to be serious.

"Sister Maria Teresa would eat you for lunch. We have to get out of here before someone sees us."

Day 1. 2:00 pm, Liechtenstein Countryside

Six thousand miles away, another team assembled. They traveled from Germany, France, Austria and England. Some came in pairs, others alone, not wanting to attract attention as they made their way to the lodge nestled in the backcountry of Luxemburg. The Leader had summoned them. It was time to claim their destiny.

Under the Oval Office

Day 2. 9:00 am, White House, Washington DC

Ria Santos clutched the blue canvas briefcase as she hurried along the West Colonnade. The locked case contained "Blue Ribbon" reports too secret to send to government officials by computer. Because of her mission, she did not take her normal route, which always included a stop to marvel at the view through the stately white columns of the White House. From there, she could look out onto the Rose Garden toward the Washington Monument—the Pointy Pencil, as she called it— poking up at a distance over the treetops. Today, however, her eyes were glued to the stone tiles in front of her.

The sight of Ria bounding through the formal hall, a blur of colors from the lime green blouse to her shocking pink flared skirt, would make the most sober individual smile. It made the tall, dark-skinned woman in a plum dress entering the Colonnade laugh out loud. "Good Morning, Ria," she called out, causing Ria to come to a skidding halt just inches from the tan heels. Ria's long corkscrew curls continued to spring in all directions.

Ria looked up and caught her breath. "Omigod. Mrs. P! I mean, uh, Good Morning, Madam President."

"Good morning to you. Where's the fire?"

"Fire? No fire." Ria could not believe her luck. She had the president of the United States all to herself. What questions could she ask? "Uh, how are you and the First Husband this morning?"

"Good, Ria. Thank you. But tell me: Are you and your associate Lee getting settled? I personally supported your assignments when the Intel Center briefed me on the Junior Spy program."

"Yes, thanks Mrs. P. We're doing great. Ready to serve and protect you at all hours, ma'am."

"Not neglecting your studies?" the President asked, giving Ria the impression that she might want to double-check their homework.

"No, ma'am. We work with a tutor in the afternoons and evenings. You know we are both doing Honors programs." She and Lee were only twelve years old, but she wanted to make sure the president knew they were not slackers.

"Well, slow it down a bit, before you run somebody over." Her smile told Ria that her offense had not been federal.

"Sorry. But I gotta go. Courier duty. Excuse me." Ria

ran around the president and headed out of the West Wing into the Palm Room of the White House residence. "Good morning, Andrew!" Ria called out to the Secret Service agent on duty. Ria flashed her I.D. badge but did not stop. Andrew waived her through.

Even though Ria had been assigned to the White House staff only one month ago, everyone knew her. Her enthusiasm and habit of questioning everything had impressed almost all the staff. The exception was their supervisor, Secret Service Special Agent in Charge Duke Crenshaw.

Ria sped along the Central Hall that cut through the length of the Residence and connected the main building to the East and West Wings. The thick carpet swallowed the sound of footsteps and words while the vaulted ceiling made the hall feel like a medieval church. Ria slowed midway through the hall, where she took a sharp right turn through the North Hall to the only inside access to the basement. Instantly, the grandness of the upper floors of the White House disappeared.

The basement felt like a forgotten place, with unremarkable linoleum floors, walls in need of a fresh coat of paint, and a musty smell like just-unpacked Christmas decorations. Ria smiled and relaxed her grip on the bag.

She entered the flower shop and headed to the back, behind the tables filled with flowers and vases for the state dinner honoring the German chancellor and her husband. Ducking behind a screen, she keyed a number sequence into the cipher lock and slipped inside a secret office that most of the staff didn't know existed.

"Hey, PUZZLE-GIRL. Where have you been?" Lee Wong asked from behind a small desk with stacks of paper organized into three in boxes.

Ria grinned. She liked it when Lee used her code name. It reminded her of their work and how important it was, even when she had courier duty. She had been totally psyched when CONTROL had selected her and Lee for this assignment: Provide Intel Center support to the Secret Service and watch for anything unusual inside the White House. Although no one explained what.

She liked working with Lee the best. Sure, he looked more like a lab animal than a spy, with his pudgy belly and Coke-bottle glasses. But under his spiky black hair was one of the sharpest analytical minds Ria had ever encountered. Besides hers, of course.

"Picking up reports," Ria said. "What about you?"

"Just back from a National Security Council meeting. Biochemical threats. Nothing you'd be interested in, yet." Lee's eyes twinkled.

"Really? Try me," Ria said, leaning across Lee's desk. She always had to play twenty questions just to get the bare minimum out of Lee. "Give."

"It was nothing, really. It was just great to be included. I had to explain the scientific details to these guys. You know, it's scary. They're leading the country but don't understand the power of science. I had to draw pictures to explain the vaporization process of biological agents. They paid attention and asked my advice, and didn't even care that I'm only a kid."

That was one of the problems with the Junior Spy program. The junior part often had to be explained to adults. It was assumed that twelve-year-olds were incapable of understanding world affairs or complex theories, so no one ever suspected them of anything more devious than a prank.

The program recruited the top young minds to support intelligence missions around the globe and had existed for over a hundred years with a long history of successes. Of course, those were all secret.

Ria pulled the pile of reports from the courier bag, adding them to the chaos of paper, books, and food spread across her desk. "There are three reports marked for release. Looks like another biological weapons threat—anthrax this time."

Lee scooted his chair toward Ria. "Domestic or from overseas?"

"Montana. There aren't many details, other than it's a military weapons-grade strain, and it's been missing for at least two weeks."

Lee scanned the report. "Anthrax is a nasty biological compound. It looks just like a harmless powder, easy to mistake as baby powder or even flour. But one whiff will kill you. Germ warfare. I wonder why the anthrax report is not cleared for passage to the Secret Service? I'll call HQ to get approval."

Day 2. 9:00 am, Liechtenstein Countryside

The Leader surveyed the list of recruits, showing no sign of emotion. Emotion was weakness. Still, the Leader was pleased. The recruits were the perfect specimens of their race: strong, pure blooded, and loyal to the cause. Most of all, they were ready. Almost.

③

Museum of Flight

Day 2. 1:00 pm, Intel Center, Dulles, Virginia

Twenty-four hours and a cross-country plane ride later, Tex and Audrey exited the nondescript black car that had picked them up from Dulles International Airport in Washington, DC.

Audrey hesitated. "This can't be right. We're at the Smithsonian Air and Space Center."

"Adapt. Respond. Improvise," Tex said with a grin. "We're supposed to figure stuff out on our own. Someone will make contact with us."

As they headed for the entrance, Tex's eyes swept the area, looking for faces he knew or signs that might tell them where to go. The ka-thunk of Audrey's boots on the concrete floor next to him was sweeter than stolen honey. He was glad that he was teamed with her. She was the last person anyone would suspect of being a spy, especially with those hot pink cowboy boots.

The museum was already crowded with sightseers, but that didn't stop Tex from immediately spotting MOLECHECK standing behind the information desk in the lobby. Their fuzzy redheaded spy school mentor gave no sign of recognition when he saw Tex. MOLECHECK just turned and headed down the hall at a fast clip, forcing Tex and Audrey to jog to keep up with him. For eight weeks, MOLECHECK had overseen every aspect of their training. He could be tough, but he stood up for them when it counted.

MOLECHECK stopped at an elevator and glanced behind Tex and Audrey for just a second. Tex recognized the classic counter-surveillance move. MOLECHECK was making sure no one was following them.

The three of them stepped into an empty elevator at the end of the hall. Tex was not surprised when he felt MOLECHECK slip something into his hand. It was a badge that identified him as museum staff.

The elevator panel had two buttons, one for the main floor and another for the observation tower, located 164 feet above. The tower was popular with tourists, as it offered a 360-degree view over Washington Dulles Airport and the surrounding area. MOLECHECK ignored the buttons and swiped his badge through an optical scanner at the base of the panel. The elevator immediately dropped. Tex felt Audrey lean into him, shaking and nervous as a fly in a glue pot. Audrey did not like elevators.

After a fast but long descent, the doors opened onto a well-lit lobby with a seal inset into the marble floor: an American eagle with a key and a scroll gripped in its talons. Tex felt the thrill of stepping into Intel Center HQ for the first time.

The director of the Junior Spy program greeted Tex and Audrey. Gone were the camp clothes. She looked like a corporate raider in her tailored black pinstriped suit, not a spymaster.

"Howdy, CONTROL," Tex said with a grin. "Where are Lee and Ria?"

"I didn't bring you back for a reunion. You are expected in the Briefing Room."

Tex shrugged, same old CONTROL. All business.

Tex and Audrey followed CONTROL into a glass-enclosed room with an oval conference table and twelve chairs. At one end, there was a large TV monitor on the wall, at the other end, an LCD map of the world with flashing lights; some red, others green. Tex noticed that most of the red ones were in Africa and Europe.

"Agents LAB-MAN and PUZZLE-GIRL have been deployed on another mission," CONTROL announced. "Your missions are bigoted, meaning you do not have a need to know about what they are doing, nor they, your mission. That should answer any other questions."

CONTROL sat at the head of the table, her back to the LCD map. She pointed Tex and Audrey to chairs on either side of her. At each place rested a thick folder marked OPERATION

KILI. When Tex went to open the folder, CONTROL clicked her tongue, stopping him.

"This briefing is on Operation Kili," CONTROL began. "Security classification Top Secret. Listen and I will take questions at the end of the briefing."

The lights in the room dimmed as an image appeared on the TV screen in front of them. The image looked like it had been taken from a long distance and magnified several times. It was dark and blurry with rows of whitish blobs.

"This is a mountaineering camp at the base of Mt. Kilimanjaro located near the town of Arusha, in Tanzania. It's registered to Dik Dik Climbs and Safaris International." The next image showed a close-up view of black and white tents.

CONTROL's voice tensed. "There has been an influx of young climbers, mostly European, in the last month. The permit process for the Kilimanjaro National Park has been expedited for these youth groups, keeping other climbers off the mountain. The number of climbers on the mountain at any one time is strictly controlled. We believe someone is paying a large sum of money to the Tanzanian National Parks Department—as well as the guides and porters—to hide the activities of this camp from authorities."

"Since when did mountain climbers become so interesting to spies?" Tex asked.

CONTROL's eyes flicked from the screen to Tex, sharp as a cowboy's spur. She clicked to the next slide.

"They are of interest since we discovered their gear is not just hiking poles and camp supplies." The next image showed a stack of crates, the top one open. Inside, matte black rifles were stacked in two piles.

Audrey shifted in her seat. "For hunting?" she asked, disgust written across her face.

"Semi-automatic rifles are not a sportsman's rifle. We suspect that this is some type of a military training camp for youth."

CONTROL flicked on the lights. "Your mission is to infiltrate this camp and collect intelligence on the identity of the organizers and purpose of the training. We need to know who they are and what they are planning. With weapons involved, you need to take extreme care. If you accept this assignment, you must know that you'll be out there on your own, with no one to bail you out if you get into trouble."

Tex exchanged glances with Audrey. She was twisting the medallion necklace she always wore around and around, tightening the chain to a choking point before untwisting it again. She furrowed her brow and clenched her lips tightly.

"Understood," Tex said with a curt nod. No one was going to make him or Audrey buzzard bait.

Day 2. 1:00 pm, Liechtenstein Countryside

The Leader acknowledged the rap on the door with an order to enter. It was First Lieutenant Frederick, who stood at attention just inside the doorway. The Leader remained seated and did not return the salute.

"The last squad is ready to depart. I will accompany them."

The voice matched the young man, low and muscular. He wore a black shirt and pants, which fit tight over his bulging frame. His face was square and topped with a razor-sharp stubble of blond hair.

"You have checked each one?" the Leader asked, not waiting for a reply before returning to the roster on the desk.

"Yes, personally."

"They are well versed in their cover for the trip?"

"Yes. I have tested each one and am satisfied they will play their parts correctly, just as the earlier squads have done."

The Leader grunted. If the lieutenant was satisfied, that should be good enough. The details, the smallest of matters, could lead to failure. Six months had been spent perfecting the plan. "Failure is not an option."

The lieutenant stood taller, his pale eyes unblinking. "My men are prepared to die to achieve our mission. We will not fail you."

"There is no sacrifice too great. Each one of us must be ready to die. Are you, Frederick?"

"Yes, my Leader." Frederick snapped his heels together and gave another salute.

The Leader nodded in approval. "You are the vanguard. Only if you succeed will the others, weak and confused by the lies of the sub-humans, find the courage to follow. You are dismissed."

The Leader returned to the papers but the lieutenant remained in the room. "Is there something else, Frederick?"

"The Americans. When should I expect them?"

"You see to your charges. I'll take care of the Americans." The rebuke caused the lieutenant to flinch, only slightly but enough to hint at his unease. He might have thought the Leader did not completely trust him. This was true, but it was not the only reason the Leader had kept silent about the Americans.

16

4

Bossy Business

Day 2. 2:00 pm, White House, Washington DC

Ria logged the Top Secret reports into the computerized tracking system and prepared the read-board for Special Agent in Charge Crenshaw. Ria and Lee worked for Intel Center, but for this assignment, they reported directly to Crenshaw, something that Ria had liked at first, until she met him. In addition to the Top Secret Blue Ribbon reports, there were eight less sensitive ones that had come into her secure in-box during the morning. Only government officials with Top Secret security clearances could read them and only if they had a need to know.

Paperwork completed, Lee and Ria headed upstairs to meet with Crenshaw. Lee carried the blue canvas case. Crenshaw's office was on the ground floor of the West Wing, located directly under the Oval Office.

The Secret Service offices were three times as large as Lee and Ria's basement cubbyhole and were richly decorated with dark wood paneling, plush carpets, and expensive furniture. The main room smelled of patchouli and vanilla, not musty one bit. Crenshaw's secretary, Mrs. Werner, had a tidy desk near the door, which was oddly organized in twos. There were two phones, two computer monitors, two desk lamps, two candy dishes, and two photo frames. Each picture had two people in it: Mrs. Werner and someone else. The desk chair— only one—was empty because Mrs. Werner was on vacation.

The door to Crenshaw's private office was closed. Ria and Lee took seats on one of the sofas. As usual, Crenshaw kept them waiting, first talking on the phone and then meeting with two Secret Service teams assigned to protect the vice president and his wife.

Ria was good at many things. Waiting was not one of them. "Why does he always do this to us?" she whispered to Lee as she fidgeted in the deep leather couch. Her feet didn't touch the ground, and it made her feel even smaller than she was.

"He's a busy guy. He's responsible for the security of the president and all these important White House officials."

"Yeah, but he treats us like we're kids."

"We are kids," Lee whispered back, giving Ria a look that only made her madder.

"Why are you always standing up for him?"

"Shush," Lee said, keeping his voice low. "I'm not. I just

think that you're overreacting."

"Overreacting!" Ria stood up and headed for the candy dishes on Mrs. Werner's desk. "How long has it been? Half an hour?" Ria didn't lower her voice this time.

"If you don't like the wait, leave the folder and pick it up later," boomed a voice from within the inner office.

"You know we can't do that," Ria hollered back.

"Ahem." Lee cleared his voice, shooting Ria a warning look. "What my colleague meant was security regulations DCID 6/4 and 6/9 require that we keep Top Secret reports in our physical control at all times. No exceptions, sir. If you want us to come back at a better time—"

"There's never a better time," Crenshaw grumbled as he appeared at his door. "Who do you think you are to quote regulations to me?" Crenshaw added. "D-skid whatever." Six feet tall, square-jawed with shoulders the size of a Humvee, even Ria had to admit Crenshaw cut an impressive figure. That was until he opened his mouth. "Let me have the bloody reports."

Lee unlocked the courier case and handed Crenshaw a sealed envelope. Grunting, Crenshaw broke the seal and flipped through each report, scanning the small print as he continued grumbling under his breath. "Why do you bring me this dribble? There's nothing here even remotely relevant to the president's security."

"You might want to take a second look at the report on the missing anthrax culture. The lab is in Montana. Last week, we had another odd report about militia groups organizing in that same general area," Ria said, working hard to keep her voice even.

Lee added, "This particular anthrax sample would make a very deadly biological weapon."

"Do you have anything to connect the reports to each other or to the president?"

"No, sir, but it's my assessment that—"

"You're wasting my time."

Crenshaw threw the Top Secret documents at Ria's feet and disappeared into his office. "You're dismissed!" he bellowed through the open door. In a slightly lower voice, but still loud enough to be heard all the way down the hall, he added, "Why do they send me kids?"

Day 2. 3:00 pm, Moshi, Tanzania

Dr. Mawanzi examined the two bodies. They had been dead for four hours. There was nothing he could do, except make another report. The two climbers were young and fit, just like the others. They had died of altitude sickness.

The Ministry had been perfectly clear on the protocol for such unfortunate events. The deaths would be kept quiet. Tanzania depended upon tourism. If visitors knew the true dangers of climbing...

5

Bugging Out

Day 2. 3:00 pm, Covert Intel Center Jet

"Take your seats and buckle up," the captain announced over the intercom.

The spy plane did not have normal rows of seats. Audrey secured herself into a specially configured workstation across from Tex. The engines started up and the Intel Center plane did a short taxi among the Air and Space Museum's historic planes on the runway before four super-powered jet burners sent it skyward seconds later.

Audrey was worried. In the rush to catch the plane from San Francisco, she forgot to pack her hairdryer and special face soap. Now she was going to look like a total mess for her first mission. She had never been to Tanzania before, but she suspected that acne soap would be hard to come by. Audrey took out her compact and peered into the tiny mirror. No problem yet.

"I'll trade you," MOLECHECK said, interrupting Audrey's self-inspection. MOLECHECK leaned against the desk for support as the airplane bounced through the air. He held a manila envelope with her code name. Audrey immediately dumped the contents, shaking it a few times for good measure. She had a watch with more than the normal number of dials, which turned out to be a compass and GPS. A nail file/lock pick set, a small breath freshener that was really pepper spray, and a miniature flashlight concealing a tiny camera.

MOLECHECK handed her a flat metal container, small enough to fit in her palm.

Audrey pressed a button on the side and the top popped open to reveal a mirror and lip gloss. "Thanks, I think." She had learned to be wary of MOLECHECK's gifts. They usually contained something unexpected. "What is it?"

"Lip gloss," MOLECHECK said, eyes twinkling.

"And?" Audrey asked.

"And an encrypted text messaging system."

MOLECHECK knelt down next to Audrey and began showing her the buttons she needed to hit in order to use the electronics.

"Will COW-BOY get one of these?" Audrey asked, laughing.

"Yes," MOLECHECK said. "His is hidden in an electronic translator. Tex, do you want to swap?"

"No, thanks. Not my color," Tex said. "What else do you have for us?"

"Disguises. Follow me."

Waiting by the restrooms was VIOLET, their spy school disguise master. She too had transformed her look since summer. She wore a stretchy black bodysuit, making her look sleek and catlike, except for the red high-top sneakers. Audrey winced. VIOLET scared her. It wasn't that she was mean, but you just never knew when something would set her off and she would transform into a screaming psycho. Audrey managed a weak "hi" before taking cover behind Tex.

But VIOLET wasn't going to have any wallflowers. "I've got disguise kits and alias documentation all ready for you."

Audrey took the small box marked with her code name, MIND-READER. Inside she found a passport, library card, and Sierra Club card, all in the name of Allison Bayer, resident of Colorado Springs, Colorado. The passport was missing a photo. The box also included a pair of dark-rimmed glasses which looked oddly like the ones worn by Sister Maria Teresa and a box of hair color: dark blonde. She checked the label again. Yep, it was dye. "There must be a mistake."

"That's not a mistake, dear," VIOLET said sweetly, giving Audrey a not-so-gentle push toward the bathroom while handing her a large, dark towel. "Wigs don't work in Africa. Too hot. You'll thank me later."

Audrey gave her pretty golden-red ponytail a last look. Thirty minutes later, she was indeed transformed. Along with the glasses, the look said "ugly teenager." She was angry, then terrified. What if the dye never came out? What if she had hair the color of dirty dishwater when she went home? How would she explain this? She'd just stay in the bathroom the rest of the flight. No, the rest of her life.

"You're burning daylight, Aud." Tex banged on the door. "MOLECHECK is waiting for us." She ducked her head, opened the door, and raced up the aisle.

"Is that you?" Tex said sitting down next to her. "Wow, I'd never recognize you. Great disguise."

Tex had sprouted long, shaggy hair and wore a tie-dyed shirt. He had an earring in his right earlobe. She pushed up her Sister Maria Teresa glasses. Had that been there before?

MOLECHECK cleared his throat. "Back to business? We don't know very much about Dik Dik Climbs and Safaris. They do not have a registered office in Tanzania. Their Liechtenstein address is an empty office, probably just a mail drop. In the spy business, we call this a front, and it's a telltale sign of some sort of illegal activity."

Audrey nodded, searching her memory for details on Liechtenstein. It was a tiny country, next to Switzerland. She had visited it once, to go skiing.

"For Operation Kili, we will be landing in Dar es Salaam, the capital of Tanzania," said MOLECHECK. "You'll take a bus to Moshi. Your mission is to find Dik Dik Climbs and join them. Be discreet. We don't want to signal our interest. I'm worried about those weapons and something else."

"What?" Tex asked, not sounding the least bit worried.

"Over the past month, there have been an unusually high

number of deaths among climbers on Kili. You need to be very careful."

Audrey swallowed. Could they be headed into a camp of killers? She unconsciously grabbed her necklace and began to twist.

Day 2. 8:00 pm, Bitterroot Valley, Montana

Three American teens rode in silence on the long, windy mountain road. It was late, the weather stormy. The eighteen-year-old drove. His two younger passengers dozed, one in the passenger seat, another in the back.

They were late. At this rate, they'd miss their flight. The Boss would be angry. He pressed down on the accelerator, taking the curves more quickly. The wheels squealed a little. Better not make the Boss mad.

He glanced at the kid in the passenger seat. For a sixteen-year-old, he was big. He wore a cowboy hat pulled down over his eyes. Before yesterday, he had never set eyes on these guys. But the Boss said they were good, maybe even better than he was. Yeah, like that was even remotely possible. No one could outrun, outfight, or outshoot him.

Movement along the side of the road caught his eye. He hit the brakes. A stag and two does bounded from the trees. He braked harder, the car shimmied and spun. The last thought the driver had before the car plunged into the ravine was the Boss was going to be really, really mad.

6

Ink Blot Test

Day 3. 11:30 am, White House, Washington DC

Lee stabbed the ice pick borrowed from the White House kitchen into the bottom of a Styrofoam cup. Rotating the pick in a circular motion, he continued to widen the hole until he was satisfied it was big enough. With great care, he pulled a fountain pen out of a plastic bag and placed it tip up into the Styrofoam holder.

Lee lowered safety goggles over his glasses and adjusted the plastic apron to protect his shirt and tie. In one month, he had already ruined two ties. Dressing up was one drawback to this job. Kids and scientists should not have to follow the White House dress code.

Lee pushed down on the writing tip and then moved away. He made a note of the time, to the exact millisecond. Then he waited. A minute ticked by. Then another. Lee checked his watch. Why was the pen inert? Something had gone wrong with his design.

He pulled up a stool and settled in, elbows resting on the florist's table. He cradled his head in his hands and kept his eyes level with the top of the pen. He figured he must have made some sort of miscalculation on the amount of time needed for the chemical action to create sufficient pressure to reverse the effects of gravity on the ink.

This was not his first prototype using a pen, but the others were for fun, not spy craft. They made great practical jokes. Lee loved playing jokes on others, especially when he could use his scientific knowledge to create really awesome pranks. No one ever suspected him, because they all thought he was too nerdy to have a sense of humor. That made the joke even sweeter.

The pen sputtered. Lee checked his watch. Seven minutes, twenty-one seconds. No, not sputtered, Lee decided on closer examination. Dribbled. From the tiny holes near the top of the pen, black ink began running down the sides of the pen.

It had to be a more forceful reaction to work with Spy Dust. Lee was experimenting with ink because Spy Dust was invisible to the naked eye. It would be too hard to measure and time each spray with an invisible substance. Lee had been experimenting with different Spy Dust concealment devices that could be planted on suspect agents. The pen would shoot out the Spy Dust at regular intervals, creating a trail, which could be seen with ultraviolet light.

The pen sputtered again. Lee jotted down the time. The interval was right, three minutes, but the spray distance was less than before. Some inventor he was. Only in his dreams would he ever be the guy everyone turned to in the moment of crisis and scream for him to save them. When CONTROL summoned him last month and told him about this assignment, he was excited. But that was before he found out CONTROL had a different assignment for Tex, probably one with real danger and excitement. The most danger he faced was a paper cut.

The pen sputtered once, twice, then exploded. Ink drilled into his forehead, goggles, and nose.

"Sweet Einstein," Lee shrieked.

Ink filled his mouth. Blinded and coughing, he reached up to remove the goggles. The lights were back on, but he wished they weren't. The White House florist was going to kill him. Ink peppered the walls, worktables, and floors. The pretty white flower arrangements for the president's tea now had more of a Dalmatian theme.

His coughing switched into wheezing as he fought for each breath. Panic and musty rooms were a bad combination for his asthma. He took a hit from his inhaler and tried to relax. Then he did the only thing he could. He grabbed a roll of paper towels and swabbed the deck.

An hour later, Lee collapsed into his chair inside the small office he shared with Ria. He had managed to remove most of the ink, even from the ceiling, but some things were beyond repair. Rose pedals don't like to be scrubbed. He ended up dumping the flowers into the burn bag with the soiled apron and safety goggles. Better the florist should face a mystery than know the truth.

Would there be an investigation? The case of the missing flower arrangements? Would they interrogate everyone? He imagined Special Agent in Charge Crenshaw towering over him, issuing threats to confess or else. The thought made him laugh so hard he fell off his chair. That was when Ria found him.

"What happened to you?" she demanded.

Lee could only laugh harder, his belly pitching from side to side. He gasped for breath, but couldn't stop.

"Look at yourself," Ria said. She pulled out a compact.

Lee saw his reflection and let out an even louder roar. His face was completely black, except for the area around his eyes, where the outline of the safety goggles was clearly marked.

"What have you been doing?"

"I was attacked by a killer fountain pen."

"Yeah, and it's clear who won."

Day 3. 5:00 pm, Liechtenstein Countryside

The Leader's impatience was growing. The American should have called by now. It was clear from the beginning that Barry VanderCourt would be a problem. Still, they needed VanderCourt's network for the American uprising to succeed. First America, then Europe, then the world. When VanderCourt was no longer useful, he could be killed if necessary.

The phone vibrated. "You're late," the Leader said.

"Perhaps." The vowels were long and drawn out, speaking to VanderCourt's origins in the American West.

"Well?"

"Well what?" boomed VanderCourt.

The Leader's blood boiled. If the man were here, he would learn the cost of not showing proper respect. The Leader gripped the phone to calm the rage. "The last of my recruits are en route. Have yours left?"

"They will be there soon enough," said Vandercourt. "More importantly, where is my shipment?"

There was something peculiar in his answer, a momentary pause before the words 'soon enough'. "Is there something I should know," asked the Leader.

"You should know where my shipment is. If you expect me to test the goods before we use them, I need them and now."

The Leader sighed inwardly. It was true. "The goods will be delivered to the warehouse on Sunday night. When will your—" But the line was dead. The American had hung up. The Leader swore but then stopped. Emotions were for the weak. There was no time to waste. There was a plane to catch.

7

Welcome to Tanzania

Day 4. 10:00 am, Moshi, Tanzania

"Welcome to Moshi," the Tanzanian bus driver said as he opened the doors letting in a blast of African heat.

They had made it through immigration without being challenged and caught an early morning microbus to the town at the base of Mount Kilimanjaro.

All Tex wanted now was some fresh air. The place reeked of body odor and something worse. He was ready to barf up his socks. After two days of nonstop traveling, he needed to get off his butt and work his lungs. Tex bolted off the bus at the first chance.

"Do you have the map of Moshi?" Tex said to Audrey as they started walking.

Audrey dropped her pack and began removing items, one by one. Out came five books, a camera, some clothes, a Ziploc bag full of toothpaste, a picture of the Golden Gate Bridge, and some seashells.

"What's all this?" Tex asked, poking at the shells.

"Just the essentials. I can't seem to find my map, though." She rooted around a little more in her bag. "Never mind, I memorized most of it. I think."

Tex pulled a crinkled map out of his pack and a list of travel agencies, marveling at Audrey's definition of essentials.

"This shouldn't be too hard," Audrey said, bag repacked. "How many travel agents are there? Two? Three?"

"There's twenty-one on the list."

"Twenty-one?" Audrey squeaked. "We could just ask some climbers if they've heard of Dik Dik Climbs." She nodded toward a group huddled together under the shade of an acacia tree.

"No," Tex said firmly. "Bad tradecraft." Spy school had drilled into them the special ways spies work, to keep their operations secret.

"Maybe we should split up." Audrey took the map from Tex. She rotated around, making two complete circles. "Whoa, dizzy. I'll go this way," she pointed left, "And you go that way."

Tex shook his head. Letting Audrey roam alone did not sound like a good idea. While he had confidence in Audrey in many areas, map reading was not one of them.

The bus had let them off in the center of town. Shops spilled out onto the sidewalks with trays of souvenirs perched on small wooden stools. It was difficult for two people to pass without one knocking into a store display or falling off the elevated curb. The smells of coconut and cabbage mixed with spices reminded Tex that they hadn't eaten in a while. Their flight to Africa had been close to sixteen hours. Maybe some food would settle his nervous stomach.

"You hungry?" Tex swung around, almost taking Audrey out with his pack.

Audrey did a quick pirouette to avoid a direct blow to the head. "Kind of. But don't you think we should find the Dik Dik office first?"

"No, first we need to see if anyone is following us." Tex nodded toward a crooked-nosed man loitering in the square who had been on the same bus with them.

They hefted their packs, and Tex headed for a narrow alley tucked between two souvenir shops. In just a few steps, the noise and bustle of the main street disappeared into a labyrinth of back passages. When they were certain no one was following them, they circled back into a small courtyard filled with tables with blue and white striped umbrellas. Lush vines of bougainvillea with little purple flowers climbed along the walls of the courtyard creating a shady oasis.

Audrey ordered in a musical language he did not understand. Magically, two sodas and a pile of Samosa meat pies appeared in front of him.

"Where did you learn to speak like that?"

"Swahili? The guidebook," Audrey said, nibbling on her hand-sized pie.

"When?"

"It was a long plane ride." Audrey smiled sweetly. "And I only learned what the book called 'Useful Phrases.' Like ordering food, names of animals, and my favorite, *haraka haraka haina baraka.*"

"What's that mean?" Tex shoved a pie in his mouth and chewed.

"Hurry, hurry has no blessing."

Tex laughed through an overstuffed mouthful.

"Did you know that dik-diks are tiny antelope? When they run, they go super-fast and in a zigzag pattern while making this cute noise through their nose as a warning. It sounds like dik-dik. That's how they got their name."

Audrey sat up straight, extending her face upward and made a clicking sound, trying to imitate a dik-dik.

"Knock of off, Aud," Tex said. "People are staring." The truth was he liked her crazy sense of humor. He pretty much liked everything about her. Not that he'd ever let her know.

Audrey slumped in her chair and reached for her necklace. "Do you think the human dik-diks will be as hard to catch as the animal kind?" she whispered.

"C'mon Aud," Tex said. "It's our first mission. It's going to be slick as a whistle. So let's get a wiggle on before the shops close for lunch." As he got up to leave, he stuffed the remaining three Samosas in his mouth.

Audrey followed him, carefully wrapping her uneaten samosas in a paper napkin.

Tex led them back into the alley maze. The smells, heat,

and crowds made him regret eating so fast.

"I still think we should split up," Audrey said, adjusting her pack from side to side.

Tex groaned. "The last thing I need is for you to get lost." He wiped the sweat off his brow. When did it get so hot? He tried and failed to focus his eyes on the list of travel agents.

"I'm not the one who'll get lost," Audrey protested.

A large belch escaped Tex lips, followed quickly by another. "Pardon you?"

Tex stopped listening as his stomach lurched. The final three meat pies were grumbling at the bottom of his stomach like nasty green apples.

He dropped his pack and dove toward a metal trash barrel. Tex heaved as chunks of samosas spewed out, coating him and the barrel in a sticky, sour-smelling mess.

"Ewwwww," Audrey said from behind.

Tex groaned and barfed again. He wiped his mouth with the paper in his hand.

"Gross. You threw up on our list!"

"Can't you see I'm dying here?" Tex mumbled. "I need to lie down."

He reached out for Audrey to steady himself, but she scooted away.

"You stink."

"I could use some sympathy," Tex groaned as he stumbled back to his pack and sat on it. Using the front of his shirt, he wiped his face. When he looked up again, Audrey was gone.

Day 4. 10:00 am, Missoula County, Montana

The ambulance pulled away, leaving behind two sheriff cruisers and a flatbed tow truck. The car was too damaged from the plunge into the ravine to be towed by a regular truck. The roof was crushed into the passenger area; the trunk had been pushed forward obliterating the backseat. The driver and two passengers would have died instantly.

"Hey, Bud," called one of the sheriffs from inside the patrol car. "Come look at this."

Officer Bud Schultz slid into the passenger seat and looked at the screen with the results of the vehicle license plate search. "Hmm, stolen."

"Guess they were going for a joyride and lost control."

"Maybe, but why go for a joyride with your passports and airline tickets? Did you get anything on their names?"

"Nothin' yet. Still working on it."

"Kids. And too young to die," Officer Schultz said, shaking his head.

"Yeah, seem kinda young to be heading off by themselves to Africa, too."

8

Montana Militias

Day 4. 10:00 am, White House, Washington DC

The pipes overhead hissed and knocked, sending little puffs of steam and droplets of water onto the desk below. The heat had finally been turned on in the White House. While Ria was relieved that she would no longer need to wear the wool cap that smashed her wild curls, the old steam heating system filled their basement office with a funky smell.

"It smells like wet dog," Lee said from the doorway, wheezing loudly. Faint beads of sweat glistened on his brow. "Do you think it's going to be like this all winter? I'll suffocate. I'll die." He flopped into a chair next to her desk, flapping the ends of his button-down shirt to cool himself.

"Hey, where did you get that?" Lee reached for a pastry

sitting on Ria's desk.

"The cook likes me. I make him laugh." Ria tried to rescue part of her pastry, but Lee escaped by pushing his chair across the concrete floor. He slid hard into his desk. "Oooffffhhh," he said through the pastry crammed in his mouth.

A low beep alerted Ria to an incoming e-mail. Ten messages downloaded in quick succession. Scanning for anything she needed to pass on, Ria moved the e-mails into colored-coded folders on her desktop. Red for urgent, blue for her boss's review, and yellow for the watch list. Each day for the past month, she and Lee had been reading dozens of reports. She found them interesting, even if Crenshaw did not.

Ria skimmed one on a barbecue at a private ranch in Bitterroot Valley, Montana, hosted by the Rough Riders, along with a video clip about self-made millionaire Barry VanderCourt. He had built an 8,000 square-foot log house and guest retreat compound outside of Bitterroot Valley. In recent months, he had become a regular fixture in Washington, hosting fundraisers and pushing for pet causes.

She stopped to examine the photos. The mansion had been featured in a recent issue of Traditional Homes and Estates. There were horse paddocks, well-stocked fishponds, and rare animals for hunting. Barry's wife posed with two snow-white poodles, in a room filled with eighteenth-century French antiques. Ria smiled, comparing Mrs. VanderCourt to her pets. They all wore diamond collars and their hair was piled high. It was amazing how dogs look like their owners.

A picture at the bottom showed millionaire Barry leaning

against an all-terrain vehicle, a rifle resting across his knee. It wasn't until Ria got to the third e-mail that her mind started to see the puzzle pieces coming together.

"Agggghhhh!" Lee whined as he pushed his computer monitor to a corner of his desk away from a growing puddle of water.

"I'm trying to concentrate here. Can you keep it down?" Ria started a new search. She knew she was fishing blind, but there seemed to be one too many reports on activities in remote parts of Montana. The Crime page of the *Bozeman Daily Chronicle* mentioned a recent gun show, where several dealers had reported the combined loss of over twenty-five automatic weapons. Security had been tight, and no one was allowed to leave the grounds without proper paperwork and a gun permit. It was an inside job, but no one was talking.

"What do you know about extremist militia groups?" Ria scooted her chair toward Lee.

"They like guns and are really paranoid."

"What else?"

"They think they are above the law. They hate the government, and they like to live in hard-to-get-to places."

"So why would they work together?"

"They wouldn't."

"Then why are they planning a weenie roast?"

"They're hungry?" Lee's stomach growled on cue. It was almost lunch.

"Seriously, I have been sitting here all morning staring at a screen until my eyes are crossed, trying to find a connection.

That's the best you can give me?"

"Write it up and give it to Crenshaw if you think it's so important," Lee said, cautiously poking a pen stuck into a Styrofoam cup.

"Well, one of us needs to show our program does important work." She stuck her tongue out at Lee, but he was too absorbed to notice.

Ria gathered her facts into the official report format preferred by Crenshaw. Maybe this time he would be impressed with her work.

Fifteen minutes later, Ria walked into the Secret Service offices. Mrs. Werner, Crenshaw's secretary, welcomed Ria with a smile and a strong scent of patchouli and vanilla.

Ria was in a hurry, but she remembered MOLECHECK's lesson on the importance of good manners. Spies need to get people to like them if they expect to get help. "Hi, Mrs. Werner. How was your vacation?" Ria asked.

"Hi hon, nice, but too short. You're looking sharp today," Mrs. Werner said, admiring Ria's bright blue sweater. She held out a box of Swiss chocolates. "I brought these back. Take one for you and Lee."

"Thanks, but I should see Special Agent Crenshaw first," Ria said.

"He's on the phone, sweetie. He's had a long morning and is not in the best of spirits." Mrs. Werner added the last part in a half-whisper. She used a pencil to tuck a wisp of white-blonde hair back into her messy bun and gave Ria a wink.

Ria was about to thank her for the tip when Crenshaw

bellowed at her to come in. Ria made a mental note that his hearing was as sharp as his bite. She bet Mrs. Werner didn't want to come back from vacation because of Crenshaw.

Crenshaw motioned for her to approach his desk. With the phone pressed between his ear and shoulder, he snatched the envelope without so much as a thank you. He tossed it in his in-box and motioned for her to go. Ria sighed. Maybe after reading her assessment he'd realize that she was more than a delivery girl.

Day 4. 11:00 am, Undisclosed Location, USA

The Leader's phone vibrated. Caller I.D. read Unknown. Only five people had this number: two were dead, one was in Africa, one in Montana, and that left only one possibility. "Yes?"

"Hello, my friend."

It was Viktor. The Leader had been waiting for his call. Viktor Gordieski was a professional and punctual. "You have news?"

"Yes," the Russian arms merchant said. "Your cleaning supplies have been delivered."

"To which location?"

"Both. And now for my payment—"

"Once my men have inventoried and verified the quality of the supplies, your bank will receive the transfer," said the Leader.

"You don't trust me?" the Russian snarled.

"I don't trust anyone. Just like you, my friend."

9

Dik-Diks

Day 4. 11:00 am, Moshi, Tanzania

Audrey dashed down the alley, concentrating on the familiar landmarks leading back to the main square where she had seen two souvenir shops. She had made a rhyme to remember the series of left and right turns. Sure enough, with a final *haraka baraka left-ti-ka home*, Audrey emerged from the alley.

She grabbed a T-shirt hanging in the entryway of the shop and paid for it, using her new but cool-looking 50-shilling coin with a mama and baby rhino engraved on one side. The T-shirt was even better than the coin. Printed on the front was a white-capped mountain and underneath was its name, *Kilimanjaro*. On the back it read, *The Roof of Africa*. If that didn't make Tex feel better, at least it would help him smell less.

Audrey stepped out the shop door and smiled at the sight of her acacia tree. Silly Tex, why would he think she'd get lost?

Movement near the tree caught her attention. A group of hikers in matching shirts and pants were boarding a microbus. A rectangular sign in the front window read *Dik Dik Climbs*.

Audrey took a step forward, then stopped. She needed to tell Tex. As the last few hikers climbed on board, the bus was about to leave. She had to stop it. She sprinted across the street, toward the bus.

The door began to close.

"Wait!" Audrey hollered, waving her hands to get the driver's attention as the bus pulled out into traffic.

She ran alongside and pounded on the closed door. The driver, startled, hit the brakes. Audrey pounded again, and the door opened. She jumped inside, just as a taxi trying to pass on the right rushed by.

"Is this Dik Dik Climbs?" Audrey said, panting.

A young man with a crew cut seated in the front row responded in accented English. "Are you the American?"

Audrey blinked. "Well, yes," she stammered.

"You are alone?"

"No." Audrey's thoughts flew to Tex, sitting in his own barf. "I mean yes."

The black-shirted man stared at Audrey. Not knowing what she should say, she stared back, hoping to get a sense of him. Was he a friend or a foe?

The door swung shut behind her and the bus began moving.

"Wait, I need to—" Audrey protested. She couldn't mention Tex because she had just said she was alone. But she couldn't leave him either.

"You're late. Leave your pack here." The man pointed to an empty row behind him. "Take a seat."

Flustered, Audrey did what she was told. She slid in next to the window, and a girl farther back moved up to join her. Audrey felt panic rising in her throat. She couldn't lose Tex.

The bus picked up speed as it headed out of town. Standing on the corner was Tex, his shirt dirty and his face pale. Surprised to see him, Audrey gave him the smallest of waves, his new T-shirt in her fist.

Tex opened his mouth, as if to say something and that was the last she saw of him.

Day 4. 1:00 pm, Bitterroot Valley, Montana

Barry VanderCourt convened the council of the Federation. "This is our last meeting before the launch of Phase 2. Your reports, councillors." VanderCourt looked to Roger Steiner who sat to his right around the rustic conference table.

"Media operations are on schedule," Steiner said. "Every major paper and network in the U.S. is reporting on our freedom agenda. The Freedom Federation is now a household word." VanderCourt nodded to the next man down the table.

General Stone wore the uniform and insignia of the Deputy Director of the U.S. National Guard. "I have placed our loyal followers in guard unit command positions in the major cities. Once General Watt is removed, they will follow my orders and only my orders to seize control when the time comes, if it comes." Lowering his gaze at VanderCourt, the General added, "Do you have confidence in this foreign unit? What if they fail to do the job?"

"I have been assured they will not fail. But if they cannot complete the mission, we will proceed with Plan B. Our people are moving into place. Soon we will control the Capitol Police. Regarding General Watt, be patient." Not waiting for further questions, VanderCourt turned his attention to the next seat, until all eight councillors had spoken.

⑩
Jumbles and Puzzles

Day 4. 2:00 pm, White House, Washington DC

Lee scooped up the different sections of the newspaper spread all over the basement office. He hated when Ria dissected the paper.

He kept his irritation to himself because Ria was in a mood. She was at her desk stapling reports, smacking the stapler so hard that Lee wondered if she would punch a hole in her desk. Crenshaw was the cause, having dismissed her latest report as a waste of government resources. Lee had to agree with Crenshaw that there was no proof that a militia on the other side of the country posed a threat to the president. He also kept this view to himself.

Lee opened the entertainment section and propped his

feet on his desk. He needed a break from reading the classified reports. Of course, Ria had already completed the crossword and the Jumble and had made an attempt at the Sudoku puzzle. The solution for that one was obvious. He crossed out a few of the numbers and wrote corrections on the side.

That's when he noticed a new puzzle in the lower right-hand corner, positioned under the Jumble. It was a series of letters, bunched in groups of five: There was no clue to unscramble it.

BDHIJ KAELS UTLOC XZOPT AGLIC
FITWH YAIZB FBDLD GCUXP HMLEH
EWYIK NEACC FKODF OMPGC EPOSL
NRZQP

Lee played with the letters, reordering them multiple times, seeking a pattern or at least an obvious word. His concentration was interrupted by an unwelcomed voice.

"Greetings, lowly interns." Marshall Cox stuck his head in without knocking.

Ria shot Lee a deadly look. "Who left the door open?" She flipped the papers on her desk upside down as Marshall slipped into the office.

Lee sighed. The open door was the only source of air and the constant dampness was making his asthma go crazy. With it shut, he'd just melt into a puddle of lard.

Marshall made himself at home on a chair next to Ria's desk. "What are you working on?" he asked, leaning over to look at Ria's computer screen.

Ria clicked the document closed. "First of all, it's none

of your business, so keep your hawk face out of my life and, secondly, lowly intern yourself, who invited you?"

Marshall grinned. "Even interns have a pecking order in Washington. That's why my office is upstairs."

Ria growled.

Marshall was eighteen, tall with super-long arms and legs and a nose that was in everyone's way. A senior intern, he was assigned to Crenshaw. He made sure everyone knew his family's business was politics. His dad was the governor of New Hampshire. His grandfather was the longest-serving Senator in the US Congress. Marshall grew up going to barbecues with heads of state and playing with the kids of presidents, and dear old Dad had already planned Marshall's future. There was something nice about not having to figure out the rest of your life, but then again, maybe freedom of choice and the risk of failure were still better than having someone else telling you what to do.

"Hey, you any good at solving puzzles?" Lee said, deciding to intervene before Ria tried to deflate Marshall's ego with the stapler.

"What puzzles me is what you were doing in the NSC meeting on Tuesday."

Lee groaned inwardly. How could Marshall know about that?

Ria chortled. "You can't stand that we get invited to high level meetings." Then she grinned wickedly. "Lee was briefing the principals on a weapons of mass destruction threat."

Marshall looked from Ria to Lee, doubt written across his

face.

"Actually," Lee said, looking down to hide a smile, "I was delivering donuts for the cook."

"Hardy har-har," Marshall said, faking a laugh. "Do you think I'm stupid enough to believe that?"

Ria rolled her eyes. "You seriously want my opinion?"

"I have important work to do." Marshall got up and as he passed Lee's desk, he knocked the newspaper to the floor. "Get to work," he said and walked out.

Lee picked up the paper and tossed it in the trash. He had an odd feeling in his stomach, like something was wrong. Maybe he just needed to visit the kitchen for a donut run.

Day 4. 2:00 pm, Across America

The breaking news flashing across TV screens announced the discovery of the lifeless body of the Chief of the Capitol Police behind a well-known Georgetown restaurant. He had not been seen having lunch in that restaurant, so there was no reason for him to be in the area. A colored scarf found at the scene pointed to gang involvement. A full investigation was being mounted.

11

No Longer Seeing Red

Day 4. 2:30 pm, Moshi, Tanzania

After losing Audrey, Tex checked into the Springlands Hotel under an assumed name, partly to hide, but mostly to figure out his next move.

He was sitting on the bed, typing out a message for MOLECHECK in his translator when the door to his room burst open.

"I didn't call for maid service," Tex said. "Ever heard of knocking?" He swiftly tucked the translator under his leg.

The African girl in a wild printed dress shut the door behind her and glared at him. "I'm here to clean up after *you*, not your room. MOLECHECK sent me." She spoke with a clipped British accent which surprised Tex.

"What?" This had to be some sort of a setup. How could MOLECHECK know he was there?

"When you and MIND-READER got separated, MOLECHECK figured you could use some help. I'm Agent DEAL-MAKER."

"MIND-READER?" Tex said, playing dumb.

"Check your translator. MOLECHECK has a message for you. Consider yourself checked up on, and you are now working for me."

Tex was starting to think MOLECHECK had it in for him. Why did he keep making him work with girls? He had this whole thing under control.

"I don't know what you're yakking about. Go skin your own buffalo." Tex's mind was spinning. He wasn't about to start taking orders from her.

"MOLECHECK said you'd be difficult at first." DEAL-MAKER wore a mischievous smile and looked confident. Overly confident.

"I'm not difficult," Tex shot back. "I'm here to climb a mountain."

"Yep, like me. Call me Deliah. My cover is that I'm working at the hotel. You ready to start working, or are you too busy licking your wounds?"

Tex took a deep breath. This was his first mission. He needed to pull it together. MOLECHECK was depending upon him to deliver. "I'm listening."

"Two more climbers died on the mountain."

"Falls?" Tex asked.

"No. Altitude sickness. For some reason, the climbers are not paying attention to the warning signs and heading down in time."

"Maybe they're just fixed on making it to the top," Tex said. He looked out the window. The snowy peak of Kilimanjaro was off in the distance, looking like a photoshopped postcard. Snow in Africa?

"Unlikely. Severe nausea, disorientation, and dehydration. Impossible to miss. My contacts among the guides think someone is pushing them too hard."

Her contacts? Tex scrutinized the girl. Was she trying to impress him?

"I'll let you know once I get on the mountain," Tex said.

"Not going to happen. Like I said, find me when you're ready to work." Agent DEAL-MAKER headed for the door, slamming it hard behind her. The lone picture, a view of Mt. Kilimanjaro, fell off the wall, splintering the frame and shattering the glass.

Day 4. 3:00 pm, Moshi, Tanzania

Seated near the pool with a clear view of the rooms, a man with a crooked nose tapped out a message on his phone:

Spotted the long-haired kid. Matched pic from airport. No sign of the girl. Boarded bus earlier. Will stay close but no contact. Advise if you want him picked up.

⑫
Bugged

Day 4. 5:00 pm, White House, Washington DC

Lee worked fast. His tutoring session had ended late and he only had an hour until Ria would be back in their basement office.

He had worked out a schematic the night before, using an old metal ballpoint pen for the container and a small UHF transmitter and photocell from some old electronics he had scavenged. He glued the photocell on the outside of the pen and held it in place with a State Department sticker he had found on Mrs. Warner's desk. The cell was motion sensitive, so if there was movement, it would automatically start recording.

Lee used a pair of tweezers to wedge the transmitter inside the pen and carefully screwed it back together. He had cut the plastic tube that held the ink one inch from the bottom. Just enough to make the pen work.

He would run the next phase of the experiment tonight, hiding it on the corner of Ria's desk. The receiver would be working by tonight and he would be listening to his first recording in the morning. After the test, he would try it out on bigger fish.

Day 4. 5:00 pm, Missoula, Montana

Officer Bud Schultz of the Missoula County Sheriff's Department studied the file. When he first arrived on the scene of the accident, it seemed like an open and shut case of kids driving too fast and being killed when their car went into the ravine. The weather was bad. It was dark. He'd seen far too many of these tragedies in remote parts of Montana.

The problem was the more information he got, the less the case seemed to make sense. The car was stolen from Billings two weeks prior. From the wreckage, they recovered luggage full of survival gear and airline tickets for Tanzania.

The real kicker was all three of the passports were altered. The passports were reported stolen in Austria three years ago. A memo from the FBI advised no persons on record born in the U.S. matched these names. If that wasn't enough, there was the coroner's report. One of the boys had a tattoo, a swastika. That worried him. What were good ol' boys from Montana doing going to Africa? He'd bet a week's pay that it wasn't for a safari.

⑬

The Reserve

Day 4. 5:30 pm, Dik Dik Reserve, Tanzania

Audrey clutched her pack to her chest as she climbed out of the Dik Dik bus into the fresh evening air. In the distance, the shadowy peak of Mt. Kilimanjaro was still visible. Tents sat in neat rows perched among the rocks and scrub bushes. There were more than a hundred of them. Each was identical in color, shape and tautness, just like in CONTROL's photo. It was like the hikers in the bus in their matching outfits. On the slow, bumpy ride from Moshi, they had all sat up tall and sang songs in German and French. The songs were marches, giving Audrey a surreal feeling that she had just joined the army and was going off to battle.

"Allison."

Audrey had never felt so alone.

"Allison, we need to check in and get our gear," the girl who had sat next to her on the bus said.

Audrey blinked. For a terrifying moment, she realized she was about to correct the girl, saying her name was Audrey, not Allison. But it was Allison. Allison Bayer, a student from Colorado Springs, Colorado. That was her new cover identity, and she needed to remember it, no matter what.

The girl's name was Freda and she looked to be fourteen or fifteen years old. Tall and blonde, she had the healthy farm girl look. She was German, but spoke English well. She seemed to know what to do and where to go. Audrey sensed she would attract the least notice if she stayed in Freda's shadow.

Wordlessly, Audrey followed Freda, worrying about what would happen when she was discovered. Would she be put back on the bus and sent to Moshi, or would she just disappear? This place was like no other camp she had ever been in. There was no laughter coming from the tents, just a cold silence.

Freda ducked into an unmarked tent. Inside sat a man behind a camp desk. Freda greeted him in German. Audrey, who was fluent in French from spending summers in Paris with her grandmamma, never mastered German despite her grandmamma's urgings. The man said something about the last group. He wore a black shirt and pants, which fit tight over his bulging frame. His face was square, and his blond hair buzzed short. He stopped when he saw Audrey.

A smile spread across his face. He switched to English. "I

believe the Americans have arrived. I'm Frederick; you will be taking orders from me from now on. Where are the others?"

Audrey met Frederick's eyes. She had to act like she belonged there and that if there was a problem, it was because of them, not her. She pushed her glasses back up her nose.

"That's not my business. I was told to come, and I am here." Audrey added, "Sir," not sure if she sounded too perky.

Freda shifted from one foot to another, watching Audrey. Panic swelled in her chest. She couldn't just stand there. She had to do something. She reached for the tent flap.

"Where are you going?" Frederick said with a sharp edge.

"Back to Moshi. Obviously, there has been a misunderstanding." Audrey gave a little huff and bent her head to go under the flap.

"Wait, Bayer. You need to pick up your training gear." Frederick was pointing at the metal trunks. "Pick out three pairs of each piece of clothing. Make sure you get the right size. Smalls should do for both of you."

Frederick consulted a clipboard on the desk, "Freda, take your gear to Tent 96. You and Private Bayer will share." Audrey sensed familiarity in Frederick's tone. Did he and Freda know each other?

Freda didn't wait for additional instructions, but grabbed an empty duffle bag and began stuffing camouflage gear into it. Audrey, still surprised she hadn't been thrown out, grabbed a belt, canteen, and a case with a clip. It took a moment for the object in her hand to register. It was an ammunition case. Leaning up against a wooden box were a row of semi-automatic rifles with scopes.

CONTROL had been right about the weapons. Still, it was possible this place could be a game reserve, where private parties hunted. But hunting was not illegal in Africa. So why all the secrecy? Audrey hoped she would find the answers quickly, before anyone asked her to kill something small and furry.

Audrey followed Freda in search of their tent. Sharing a tent was good and bad. She should be able to get Freda to talk about this place and why they were there. But she also would need privacy to send a message to the team. MOLECHECK had stressed they were to never use their secret communication equipment around others. She patted the compact tucked into the side pocket of her pants. It was her only lifeline to the outside world.

Day 4. 10:00 pm, Dik Dik Reserve, Tanzania

Frederick stopped typing the encrypted e-mail to the Leader. He had been told three Americans would be coming. One American had arrived, a small girl with glasses. Surely, this was not the help the Leader had promised. The Americans' mission was to coordinate with the inside contact so that Frederick's force met little resistance. More must be coming. He would get an answer. No, he would demand an answer.

Frederick paused. The Leader had not said much about the Americans. Why? Was he not trusted? Or was there another reason?

Frederick limited his report to training details and his concern that they were pushing the recruits too hard. Altitude sickness had claimed another soldier. That one was dedicated and a natural leader. He would not be easy to replace in such a short time.

⑭
Freedom Federation

Day 5. 10:30 am, White House, Washington DC

The kitchen staff was preoccupied with preparing the coffee and fresh pastries for a cabinet meeting. Secret Service Agent Palanski stood in the far corner with Todd Geringer, who worked for the vice president. The two were head-to-head, locked in a heated discussion. Todd was half Palanski's age and size but from Lee's point of view, Todd wasn't giving way to the older man.

Lee slid along the table, his eyes on the prize: glazed donuts. No one was watching as he carefully pulled one from the pile. He had his escape route lined up when a server with a heavy tray headed straight for him. Lee shoved the donut into his empty mug and ducked around the refrigerator and out of the way.

"If anyone finds out, I will make sure you're through," said a voice behind Lee. It was Todd Geringer.

"Don't worry, I've covered my tracks. You just make sure you do what I asked." Palanski's tone changed mid-sentence, and Lee felt a tap on his shoulder. "Hey kid, whatcha doing? Spying?"

"Noooo...no," Lee said, backing away. He stared at Agent Palanski for a moment. He remembered seeing him sitting in Crenshaw's office shooting the breeze, like they were friends or something. The last thing he needed was to get on Crenshaw's bad side. "I...I was looking for hot chocolate?" Lee spun around nearly missing a harried chef picking up a second tray.

"All of you! Outta here!" the chef screamed.

Clutching the smashed donut, Lee barreled through the door to their basement office, slamming it behind him.

"Where have you been? We've got a deadline."

Lee could see Ria's curls standing on end. What was with everyone today? He should have just stayed in bed.

"I'm on it."

"Well, you better have something in the next fifteen minutes."

"Scientific brain engaging. Fasten all seatbelts," Lee said muffled by the donut as he logged on. He opened intelligence reports received overnight, scanned two and found nothing. Then he opened the third. It made his brain power up a notch.

"Hey Ria, where in Montana was that the bigwig hunter guy from?"

"Bitterroot."

"I think his barbeque just got a lot more interesting. Look at this..."

Ria slid her chair over to him. Ten militia groups were coming together to form the Freedom Federation.

"Google it," Ria said.

A quick search brought up the site. It looked pretty normal at first, banded in red, white, and blue. With a click on the enter button, "America the Beautiful" began playing, as patriotic scenes, smiling families, and open pasture land floated by.

"Go to the next page." Ria reached for the mouse, but Lee was faster.

"Ria, will you just let me do it?"

A manifesto began to scroll in front of them, detailing the plans of the Freedom Federation. For once, Ria didn't poke or grab or say a single word as they begin to read:

In this time of crisis, an urgent call goes out to all true Americans to rise up and eliminate from this great nation the fifth column among us.

"What's a fifth column?" Ria said.

"I think it's us," Lee said.

Ria started to read out loud.

"...Immigrants considered inferior, who will destroy the true and majestic nature of a real America."

"Are you kidding me?" Ria shifted in her seat. "People really believe this stuff?"

"Are you kidding me? Do you ever pick up a paper?"

Both their e-mails chimed within seconds of each other. "Crenshaw," they said in unison. They were late.

Day 5. 11:00 am, Capitol Hill, Washington DC

The ceremony was a quiet affair, given the circumstances. Two sergeants at arms presided, one from each branch of Congress, the House and the Senate. The Deputy Chief of the Capitol Police graciously accepted his appointment as the new chief of the Capitol Police and immediately got to work.

Chief Griffin's first official act of business garnered praise from members of Congress. He announced the arrest of three gang members for the homicide of the late Chief of Police. What the politicians did not know was that these gang members were innocent of this particular crime. Chief Griffin felt no remorse in framing them. They were Latinos and therefore guilty by birth.

⑮

A Change in Altitude

Day 5. 11:00am, Moshi, Tanzania

MOLECHECK's message confirmed the girl was a spy. Agent DEAL-MAKER had been born in Moshi to an African mother and an American father. Probably some climber. She was recruited into the Junior Spy program several years ago and had been running missions while attending boarding school in London.

Here was the real kicker; Agent DEAL-MAKER was in charge. MOLECHECK had stressed that her knowledge of the language, the area, and the mountain would be critical. Tex groaned. He lost Audrey and now he was stuck with a control freak. What else could go wrong on his first mission?

He stood in the dust of Moshi, with large drops of sweat

rolling into his eyes. When VIOLET the disguise master had given him hair extensions, Tex had thought it was cool. Now, it was the exact opposite. It felt like a hot, wild animal hanging down the back of his neck.

"Ready?" Deliah said, appearing from nowhere.

"Sure," Tex said hotly. "MOLECHECK says you can use my help."

Deliah rolled her eyes.

"So, what's our mission?" Tex asked, jaw clenched.

"We are part of a ground support network. MOLECHECK has tasked us to case for potential agent meeting sites and an exfiltration site. All of this will ultimately help MIND-READER."

"Support network?" Tex said. "I'd just as soon bite a bug."

Deliah's face showed no emotion. "You think you're too good for it?"

"I came here to spy, not push paper."

"I'm here to save lives."

Taken aback, Tex studied Deliah. She was a cool customer. She couldn't be bullied.

"You ever lay out an improvised landing strip for a small plane?"

"Yeah, on my dad's ranch. We used a meadow."

"Brilliant," Deliah said. "We need to find and clear a strip so a small plane can make an emergency landing and leave before anyone knows it has been here. We'll need to get precise geo-coordinates so Intel Center can find it. The exfiltration site needs to look completely natural."

"What about MIND-READER?"

"What about her?" Deliah was all business, all the time.

"We can't abandon her. What if she gets into trouble?"

"Why do you think we're putting together an exfil plan?" Deliah shook her head and gave Tex a look that said he didn't know diddly squat.

Day 5. 11:30 am, Bitterroot, Montana

Barry VanderCourt called the meeting to order. Seven men and one woman seated at a rough-hewn table turned their attention to the elected head of the Freedom Federation.

"Our European partner advises Phase I of the African operation is nearly complete. It is time now for us to put the rest of our people in place for Phase 2. General Watt should receive our letter today…"

⑯

Spy Dust

Day 5. 11:30 am, White House, Washington DC

Crenshaw kept them waiting, even when they had a scheduled meeting. Lee figured it was a power trip thing. He was reminding them who was boss. Lee sunk into the royal blue leather chair, his feet stretched out in front of him. He dug his hands into the pockets of his khakis and decided this was as good a time as any to clean them out. He might actually find a piece of candy. Ria sat at the opposite end of the waiting area, thumbing through *People* magazine to pass the time.

"They have the latest edition of *Scientific America*," Lee said to save Ria from the brain-numbing publication.

Ria gave him a look usually reserved for Tex when he annoyed her, so he went back to searching through his pants.

He found his spy dust pen and smiled. He had planned on playing a prank on Ria, but needed to figure out a way that she wouldn't suspect him. Crenshaw's office was definitely not the right place. It could get both of them kicked out forever.

Continuing to rummage through his pocket, he felt something smooth and flat. He turned it in his hand. It was a 'sticky bug,' a tracking beacon you could slap on someone's back when they weren't looking.

The door to Crenshaw's office opened and out came Agent Palanski. Lee studied him as he chatted up Mrs. Werner. Palanski was a twenty-year veteran of the Secret Service. With his flattened nose and a missing left earlobe, he looked like he had had more than his share of fights. Lee remembered the heated discussion earlier between Palanski and the vice president's aide Todd. Lee wondered what he meant by covering his tracks.

CONTROL had told them to keep their eyes and ears open inside the White House. This could be important. He fingered the sticky bug. Palanski would be a good target, for both a laugh and learning if he was up to something.

Lee rose and headed to Mrs. Werner's desk. "May I get a glass of water?"

"Down the hall on your left, hon."

"I'm heading that way," Palanski said.

Lee inserted himself into the doorway just as the agent was about to pass through. He had the beacon ready, the sticky back peeled off the safety paper. Just stick it, he said to himself. "Oooffffhhh," came out of him instead as the agent continued through the door, pinning Lee against the jam. "Excuse me." Lee lurched behind Palanski and stuck the dot on the inside vent of his blazer.

Marshall Cox, know-it-all White House Intern, was standing in the hallway staring at Lee. "Hey, what are you doing?" he demanded.

"Getting some water, that is if I can walk that far." Lee tried to make a joke out of his clumsy move. "Water, water..." Lee gasped, continuing to stumble. Glancing over his shoulder, he watched Palanski, who had paused for a moment in response to Marshall's challenge, turned, shook his head in disgust and walked toward the men's room.

To Lee's horror, the sticky bug released from Palanski's jacket and fluttered to the soft, plush carpeting. Lee had forgotten that dots adhere best to natural fabrics and not poly-blends. Maybe that was why the Secret Service preferred cheap suits.

Marshall gave Lee the sign for *I'm watching you.* Then he scooped up the dot, shoved it in his pocket and walked away.

"Crenshaw's ready for us," Ria called from inside the office. "Like now."

Lee banged his head on the doorjamb. What was it with this day? Could he do nothing right?

Before Crenshaw finished reading the first report Agent Palanski returned and scooted them off the couch. He stretched out, putting his feet up on the coffee table. Lee could only imagine what Crenshaw would say if they tried that.

"Anything else?" Crenshaw said, turning his attention to

something on his computer.

"Sir, we think it's rather sensitive." Lee coughed.

"Palanski's cleared, go ahead."

"Well, in the past week, we have sent you reports showing a resurgence in militia groups. Today we have learned they are banding together as one large group, the Freedom Foundation." Lee paused for a little too long, and Ria started in.

"There is a manifesto. All true Americans are to rise up and rid the nation of the fifth column."

"What did you just say?" Crenshaw asked his full attention was on them.

"I said the fifth column, sir," Ria said.

Here it comes, thought Lee. This is when he lets loose and asks us why he must work with inexperienced kids.

"Is this just your analysis, or do you have any evidence to back this up?" Crenshaw asked instead.

"Yes, sir." Lee placed the papers on the desk.

"Thank you, you are both dismissed. Nice work."

Lee and Ria looked at each other. Nice work? They had no idea Crenshaw even knew what 'nice' meant. At least the day wasn't a total loss.

Day 5. 12:00 pm, White House, Washington DC

Crenshaw looked over at Agent Palanski. "Do you know anything about this?"

"No sir," he said. "I'll get a team on it right away."

"If any part of the Freedom Federation is true, it puts the president in grave danger. Let's keep it to ourselves for now," Crenshaw said.

"My lips are sealed," Agent Palanski said.

17

Sieg Heil

Day 5. 12:00 pm, Dik Dik Reserve, Tanzania

It had been the worst day of Audrey's life. Her shoulder ached from firing a rifle all morning. She was terrible, partly because her glasses kept fogging, but mostly because she hated guns. She had no desire to improve. She just wanted Tex to get her out of this place. Her anger flashed. He should be here, not her.

Freda asked how her day went, but there was definitely a small smile, like she already knew. Audrey just shrugged, which sent a lightning bolt of pain through her bruised shoulder and across her back.

"Don't get too comfortable, we have a rally to attend,"

Freda said.

Audrey felt trapped like one of the targets on the range today. She needed to check her messages. She needed to reach her team. Instead she did what she was told, following the other campers into the large tent. Everyone was wearing black cotton scarves tied around their necks.

At the front, a platform had been raised. Large banners in black and red streamed down along the sides. They bore a large, bold picture of an eagle. Centered on the platform, hanging from the roof of the tent was a large banner with a black swastika. Frederick walked across the stage, coming to a stop under the banner.

"The Leader's representative," Freda whispered and excitement stirred in the crowd.

Frederick waited for the room to grow silent and then saluted them, hand raised, fingers straight, locked together and pointing over their heads.

"Sieg Heil."

"Sieg Heil," the campers saluted back. Freda gave the Nazi salute and nudged Audrey to do the same. The disgust coursed through Audrey. She felt weak and nauseous. Everything was closing in on her. She couldn't breathe. This truly had to be a nightmare.

She had seen pictures of rallies like this in books. Her grandmamma had told her horror stories from her years living in occupied France, about the horrible things the Nazis had done. Instinctively, her free hand went to her prized necklace, the one she had inherited from her grandmamma. It wasn't really a necklace, but a medallion that her grandmamma was given after the war for her work with the French Underground. At night, her grandmamma was a famous Parisian singer. But during the day, she helped the resistance in the fight against the Nazis.

That was more than fifty years ago. Yet here was Audrey at this moment among Black Shirts, the new Nazi youth movement. She was now a member of their army.

Day 5. 1:00 pm, Undisclosed Location, USA

The Leader opened the e-mail, which was a mass of numbers and symbols, and selected the decrypt icon. A new window popped up, requesting a password and key. A less diligent person would have stored the key somewhere on the computer and copied the 64-digit number into the window. A less diligent person would have been caught long before. The Leader typed from memory and hit the enter button. Frederick's message, now readable, angered the Leader. Worried that soldiers were dying during training? How many times must he be told that no weakness can be allowed? Frederick must push the soldiers harder. Coddling during training would produce soft men who were not prepared to lead the new world order. The Leader's army must dominate their enemies. No one's life is more important than the mission.

⓲

I Spy

Day 5. 1:30 pm, Washington, DC

The air was crisp, requiring a warm coat, a hat, and mittens, but the sun was shining for the first day in two weeks. The continuous rains had finally let up, leaving only puddles and boggy grass that grabbed at Ria's boots and didn't want to let go. The flow of information had gone silent, and she had convinced Lee that fresh air might get their brain cells firing again.

Ria turned left at the "pointy pencil," and headed across the grass of the National Mall toward the Smithsonian Museum. She loved being back in D.C., and Lee didn't mind being a guinea pig on one of her crazy food tours. She heard the squelch, squelch, squelch of Lee's boots coming up behind her as she finished placing their first order.

"Dog with mustard, relish, and a side of popcorn." She handed Lee his food and gathered hers up along with two sodas, one tucked under each arm. They walked to a bench in front of the Castle. It was actually the Smithsonian's information center, but Ria preferred to think of it as her spot.

"Maybe we can check out the planes at the Air and Space Museum," Lee suggested.

"Muffff," Ria said. "Spicy noodles are next at the National Gallery. We only have an hour."

"How 'bout both? With ice cream? It's not like anyone will notice we're missing."

"We'll see." Ria swung her boots out in front of her as she watched a jogger go by. There were few tourists with school in session, so it was mostly government workers enjoying the break in the weather.

"Pick someone to watch, and we'll make up stories about them," Ria said.

"I spy a woman chasing a dog," Lee said.

"She's a Russian spy on a covert mission. The dog is a super-secret spy dog, trained by the enemy to retrieve information. She's on her way to make contact with another agent, when the dog grabs the thumb drive from her hand, pulls off the cap and the metal tip attaches itself to the dog's magnetized collar. Will spy dog be able to make his handoff before she catches him?" Ria said.

"That's just stupid."

"Then why's a dog heading this way?"

Before Lee could think of something to say, a beagle landed next to him and downed the rest of his hotdog in one gulp.

"I'm so sorry," the woman said returning the dog to the ground and re-attaching its leash. "Here." She reached in her pocket and handed Lee several wadded up bills. "Again, sorry."

"Looks like you're buying," Ria said, as the woman dragged the howling dog away.

"I spy a weird guy."

"We're not playing anymore. Food."

"I really spy one of our least favorite guys."

Ria followed Lee's gaze. It was Special Agent Palanski, walking across the grass with purpose in long, steady strides. There was no one else in the area at the moment, but he looked left and right, like he was searching for someone or something. He continued his route along the grass for several more minutes before turning and brushing past a garbage can, never breaking his stride before heading out to the street.

"He put down a dead drop," Lee said

"I didn't see him drop anything," Ria said.

"Exactly," Lee said. "We need to get out of sight and watch for the pick-up."

They crossed the street away from the park and stood on the sidewalk near the National Gallery.

Office workers walked the paths. No one stopped at the trash can. A flock of geese flew over, honking loudly and temporarily drowning out the traffic. When Ria looked back, the lady with the dog was nearing the can, the dog pulling hard at its leash. Ria's heart skipped. Maybe she was a Russian spy?

The beagle circled the can once. Then he squatted. What a great cover to pick up a dead drop.

"Check this out," Lee whispered.

"I am." Ria was annoyed that Lee thought she didn't get it.

"No, I mean over there." Lee pointed to a clump of trees. Agent Palanski blended in, barely visible. He was also watching the lady with the dog. The dog finished its business and pulled the lady toward the street. Agent Palanski stayed in place.

"If he put down a dead drop, why would he be sticking around?" Ria asked. "The whole point of dead drop is to pass messages without being seen together."

"Maybe he wants to see who picks it up," Lee said. "Like us."

"Or maybe you're seeing ghosts—"

Ria jumped as a hand grabbed her shoulder, spilling the rest of her soda on the sidewalk. It was Mrs. Werner.

"Mr. Crenshaw has been looking for you."

"We…we're just having lunch," Ria stammered.

"Maybe your people think it's okay to take long breaks, but the rest of us have important work to do."

Your people? Ria looked at Lee. What did she mean by that?

"Ah…Thank you, Mrs. Werner," Lee said.

They stood there for an awkward moment not moving, before Lee took Ria's arm. "We're going."

Ria glanced back. Palanski was gone and Mrs. Werner was headed straight toward the spot where they had last seen him.

Was Ria imagining things? Or was Palanski up to something? One more puzzle.

Day 5. 7:00 pm, Arlington, Virginia

The director of the US National Guard walked across the neatly trimmed grass toward the front door, not even caring if his spit-polished shoes would get dirty. It had been a long day at headquarters. The red flag was up on his mailbox, signaling a delivery.

He changed course and walked backed toward the street. The mailbox sat on a post next to the driveway and the sidewalk. Inside was one white envelope. It was addressed to Frankie Watt. Not Frank. Not Lt. General Frank Watt. Frankie. Only his mom called him Frankie, and she died over ten years ago.

The General opened the envelope with his finger, pulling out a paper folded into thirds. It was blank. The envelope was empty, except for some white powder. Was someone sending him flour?

ⓘ⑨

Hunter or Hunted

Day 6. 5:00 am, Dik Dik Reserve

Audrey ran. The dik-diks alongside her matched her graceful strides, disappearing into the grassland and then leaping into arching arabesques. Hundreds of miniature antelopes were no more than a foot tall. Crack! A high-pitched sound pierced the air, scattering the herd. She tried to keep up, but soon she was alone. Her friends had abandoned her. Fear rippled through her. Another crack. "Dik-dik! Run! Hide!" came the repeated squeaky click from the frightened creatures. A Jeep sped toward her. Standing, rifle at the ready, a black-shirted man took aim. She saw the muzzle flash and felt pain sear through her. "Die Spy," she heard him scream. She stumbled; the smell of sweet grass mixed with sweat. Her body shook.

"Wake up, Allison."

Hands grabbed her. She struggled. She must get free.

"Wake up, Allison. You're dreaming."

Audrey woke with a start. Freda stood over her with a flashlight. There was no gun. There were no dik-diks. That was yesterday's nightmare. The Dik Dik hunting safari. She didn't want to be there when it was happening, yet the memory of the frightened animals fleeing haunted her thoughts, day and night.

"Get up. We'll be late."

"Sorry," Audrey squeaked. "It must have been something I ate last night." She scrambled out of her cot and got dressed in the dark. It was another lie.

Audrey rested her head against her knee as she bent down to lace her boots. Her hand brushed against something solid. It was her compact hidden in the cargo pocket of her fatigues. It was time to phone home.

"I'm going to the bathroom. I'll meet you at the mess hall."

"You okay?"

"Just tired. I'm not sure I'm cut out for this," Audrey said, the words escaping before she could stop herself.

Freda shined her flashlight on Audrey, blinding her. "It's hard for all of us, just focus on why we are here, like we talked about at the meeting."

The meeting. That was the other half of the nightmare.

Audrey slipped out of the tent, careful of the crisscrossing lines. She headed for the outhouse, where she knew she could have some privacy. She needed to read her messages. Before going to bed she sent MOLECHECK a message about the Nazi rally, the game hunt, and the meeting last night. She was waiting for further instructions.

Slipping into the rustic outhouse, Audrey turned a block of wood to lock the door. The toilet wasn't like the plastic ones found at construction sites. It was just a sheet of plywood with a hole cut into it. The building was made of wood slats, and there was a "window" cut high to air out the toxic fumes. During the day, Mt. Kilimanjaro was visible through the tiny window. It was the only private place on the mountain.

Juggling her flashlight and the compact, Audrey punched the access code to read her encrypted messages.

Thx for readout. Clarify following:

In mtg, u were told 2 prepare 2 protect nation from inferior races. Races? Which nation? How? Military coup or terrorist operation?

U reported most recruits from Germany, France, England and Norway. Number about 150. Ages 15-25. Any other Americans?

Frederick is German and main camp organizer. Who is the Leader? Nationality? Description? Can u get close 2 him?

MOLECHECK

Frederick had led the meeting. Tall, strong, with eyes the color of the African sky, Audrey would have found him cute in any other setting. He marched back and forth in front of the seated recruits, declaring the white race superior and the world's natural rulers. It made her sick, his going on about

Arabs, Blacks, and Jews conspiring to enslave the white race. It was just about the stupidest thing she had ever heard.

She knew these words were dangerous, especially since he was also training the like-minded bigots around her to use guns. The question was against whom, and when, and where? The Leader Frederick was always talking about never appeared, but everyone talked like he was some sort of a god. Audrey had no idea how she would get close to him. She didn't even know if he was in the camp.

She resisted the temptation to finger the medallion around her neck, hidden under her clothes. If any of them saw it, she would be exposed as an enemy to their cause.

Day 6. 9:30 am, Missoula County, Montana

Officer Bud Schultz of the Missoula County Sheriff's Department was ticked. His chief refused to send the report on the three dead boys to the FBI. Chief said there was nothing federal about a random car accident.

Bud was a good cop. He had been on the force for only two years and still felt the thrill of the job. He enforced the law, was fair, and did his best every day to keep the citizens of Missoula safe. He wasn't the kind of man to disobey orders or go around his boss. But three boys with fake passports were dead, and while he couldn't put his finger on it, it just didn't feel right.

Bud waited until the chief went to lunch. He used the chief's phone to make the call.

"FBI Headquarters," a woman's voice said. "Can I help you?"

"Identity crimes, passport fraud, please…"

⑳

Operation Retrieval

Day 6. 9:30am, White House, Washington DC

Lee settled into a corner of the White House kitchen with the paper, a cup of cocoa, and a day-old donut. It was Saturday, and almost everyone had the day off. The president was traveling. There were no lunches, teas, or official events scheduled for the next few days. He liked it when nothing much was happening because it meant that he and Ria could escape and wander the halls, and give his asthma a break from the moist basement air. And best of all, Lee hadn't seen any sign of Marshall Cox, self-appointed hall monitor, for a few days.

Lee carefully rolled up the sleeves of his white dress shirt and stuffed the end of his tie inside the buttons before opening the fresh, crisp pages of the paper. He discovered the hard way that the ink on the cuffs of his shirt did not come out in the laundry.

This morning he had a chance at the puzzle page before Ria got her hands on it. He began to click the top of his pen and then stopped and reexamined it. It was his second experimental pen. One chamber was filled with regular blue ink, while a second secret chamber held spy dust.

Spy dust was made with a chemical agent called nitrophenyl pentadienal, or NPPD. There had been some controversy with the Russians using it to track American spies, and whether the chemical could cause cancer. It did make things glow in the dark when shown under ultraviolet light, but Lee was pretty sure that even if a rat glowed, it did not mean it was radioactive.

That gave him an idea. Could he make Marshall glow in the dark? Although Ria would immediately suspect him of any prank, Marshall would never figure out who did it. Lee set the pen down and went in search of another one in the kitchen.

"This is the place to work today," said Todd Geringer, the vice president's aide, causing Lee to jump in surprise. "No one knows where you are, and no one bothers you. Mind if I hide down here a while?"

Lee shook his head.

"Where'd you find the donuts, kid?"

Lee motioned to the plate with the clear domed cover.

"Chocolate sprinkles. Must have been left over from yesterday's budget committee. Conrad Wilkes's favorite."

Lee wondered if there was a reason why he kept running

into Todd. If Lee weren't a scientist, he'd think it was an omen. Geringer was young, brash, and moving his way up the political ranks at a breakneck speed. The old guard felt he had not fully paid his dues when he was tapped for this position. His support had come from a small but powerful lobby outside Washington that regularly donated large sums of money to pet causes.

There was something about Todd that rubbed Lee the wrong way. It wasn't that he didn't work hard, or wasn't bright. If Audrey had been here, she would have sensed it immediately.

Lee hunkered over the crossword, but couldn't concentrate when Todd started a one-sided phone conversation. It was "yes" and "absolutely" and "okay." Then he grabbed Lee's spy pen and jotted something down on the corner of the paper, ripped the section free and headed out of the kitchen, twirling the pen between his fingers. Lee banged his head on the counter. He would need to make a trip upstairs to retrieve the pen later, or he was going to have to make another one.

Ria slid onto the stool next to him, causing him to jump for the second time today.

"I'm bored. Nothing to do at home."

Home was the residence of Mrs. Winnie Edencamp, a short metro ride away from the White House. It was sort of like living at home, except Mrs. Edencamp was very formal. On the weekends, she taught etiquette to young Washingtonians. She seemed determined to improve Ria and Lee's manners, even though they were paying boarders, not charm school students.

"So you decided to bug me instead?"

Ria smiled at him, and then eyed the puzzle page. "The

new puzzle; can I do it?"

"What new puzzle?"

"This one." Ria pointed to the three lines of letters in groups of five. Lee had noticed it last Thursday.

"How do you solve the puzzle?" Lee asked. "There's no clue underneath, and the letters are different each day."

"Weird," Ria said. "Maybe it's just a misprint. Or a secret coded message. Like the dead drop at lunch yesterday."

"I thought I saw something." Lee was frustrated Ria did not believe him.

"So let's start pulling together the puzzle pieces."

"Okay." Lee folded the sections of the paper back together and laid it on the counter. The murder of the D.C. Capitol Police Chief covered the entire front section. The new chief promised to work with neighboring departments to put an end to gang violence by deporting members, since most were illegal immigrants.

"I'd watch out, if I were you," Lee told Ria. "Wear the wrong color scarf around the Capitol grounds and Chief Griffin will get you. That will be the last I ever hear of you."

"Ha, ha. It says illegal immigrants. I was born here."

"Do you think they'll ask before they lock us both up?" Lee teased.

Ria quietly removed her bright green and purple scarf.

"Maybe I'll just head back to visit with Mrs. Edencamp," she said, her voice hollow.

Lee hung around until dusk before sneaking down the hall to the vice president's office. Secret Service agents stood on duty outside. Lee nodded, showed his White House badge and walked past them, trying to look like he had a purpose. When, after two passes, he couldn't find Todd's office, he finally gave up and asked the agent on duty.

"The VP's staff is in the Old Executive Building."

Ria would have known this if he had only asked. Without bothering to grab his coat, Lee headed for the East exit. Once outside, he turned left and ran through the rain toward Pennsylvania Avenue. Showing his White House badge granting him high-level access to all facilities, the security guard gave him directions to Todd's office. He knew it wasn't very sneaky, but sometimes it was better to hide in plain sight.

Todd's office was on the second floor, halfway down the hall from the staircase. The door was still open, as the cleaning crew was still working their way through the building and had not locked up yet. He scanned Todd's tidy desk. Had Todd taken the pen with him? It hadn't occurred to Lee that the pen might not be here.

Lee was about to leave when he spotted an ultraviolet light. He guessed the assistant must be one of those people who suffered from Seasonal Affective Disorder or SAD, a depression brought on by the lack of sunlight during the long winters. What kind of budding scientist was he if he didn't take advantage of the light to see if the pen worked?

Lee locked the door before turning out the lights. Swinging the lamp in an arc, he began to move around the room as far as the cord would allow.

Todd must have continued to twirl the pen all the way back

to his office. There was a mark on the doorknob, across the thick carpet to the desk, and over to a file cabinet. A random group of marks covered the third drawer. Lee ran the light over the files. Near the back, he could see prints plastered all over one particular file labeled "Montana."

Intrigued, he pulled the file folder and flipped it open. Just then, the doorknob jiggled. He snapped off the light and dove under the desk, knocking over a plastic trash bin.

There was a knock, followed by a voice.

"Cleaning."

He could see feet through the small slit at the bottom. It felt like an eternity before they moved on. Climbing out from under the desk, Lee switched on the lamp and flipped through the file. Pointing his tie clip at the papers, he snapped a few quick photos then replaced the file and the desk lamp to their proper places. When he picked up the trash bin, he found his experimental pen. Satisfied that everything looked exactly as Todd had left it, minus the pen, he backed out closing the door behind him.

Day 7. 10:00 am, New York City, New York

Roger Steiner was not a man accustomed to taking orders. As the owner of a media chain, he had over 100,000 people working for him around the world. When he spoke, he expected everyone to jump. Someone wasn't jumping. Steiner wanted to know who he was and fire him. Not only would he never work in his media empire, but anywhere else. He'd make sure he was blacklisted from here to Australia and back.

Steiner's order had been simple: put the new puzzle in all his newspapers, starting last Thursday. What was so hard about that? VanderCourt asked him the same question when it didn't appear in the West Coast Sunday papers, accusing him of disobeying orders.

VanderCourt had no right to get huffy with him. They were equal partners in this operation. Without Steiner and his television stations, radio networks, Internet portals, magazines and newspapers, the Federation would have to communicate by pony express. Steiner told VanderCamp so and that shut him up. Still, a head was going to roll.

21

Evidence

Day 7. 3:30 pm, Moshi, Tanzania

Tex snapped a quick picture of the café door. At least he hoped he got it. The miniature camera was hidden in the eye of the ram engraved into his silver belt buckle, and there was no checking the shot until he was alone. He took five more of the interior, just to be covered before joining Deliah at a corner table. She tucked a small lipstick into her pocket, signaling she was finished photographing the back of the mid-sized eatery.

There were other customers nearby, so Tex kept his voice low.

"MOLECHECK sent me MIND-READER's report," Tex said. He needed to decide how much he could share with Agent DEAL-MAKER. It shouldn't include details. Maybe just that

Audrey was safe.

"Yeah, neo-Nazis," Deliah said in disgust.

Tex fumbled, spilling his coffee. MOLECHECK had told her everything?

"It's a good thing that MIND-READER and not me was assigned to infiltrate. I wouldn't have lasted five minutes."

Still off balance, Tex asked, "What do you mean?"

"Neo-Nazis hate blacks. And Hispanics, Asians, Arabs, just about anyone who doesn't believe in white superiority."

Tex leaned back in his chair and looked around the café. The crowd, mostly tourists and climbers, was a mix of ethnicities. Just like back home.

"Well, they may think they're hotter'n a pot of neck bones, but in America, that dog won't hunt."

Deliah leaned in. Her dark eyes were intense. "So you think I could come to Texas and not face any discrimination because I'm half-Black?"

"Black? No problem. But you better make sure you come legally. We've got a big problem with illegal immigrants. They sneak over the border, take all the jobs, and don't follow our laws. Their kids are citizens just because they're born here. You should see the gang problems. Hispanic gangs run drug rings, sell guns—"

"So it's just Hispanics who are a problem? And you want to throw them all out so Texas is for good white folk?"

Tex squirmed. Deliah was twisting his words, trying to make him sound like a bigot.

"I didn't say that. I'm talking about illegal immigrants."

Deliah was silent. She didn't look at him, instead poked at a small pastry in front of her. Tex was feeling uncomfortable. He thought about Ria. She was born in the U.S., but her folks were from Venezuela. Did they come to the U.S. legally? He never asked. Nor would he. Just thinking about it made him feel ashamed.

"I'm not saying we should keep all immigrants out," Tex said a little too forcefully. "Just because I think we need to fix our immigration laws doesn't make me a neo-Nazi."

Deliah met his eyes. "I'm not saying you are. But this is just the kind of issue that neo-Nazis use to gain support. They label illegal immigrants as bad people, but what they're really doing is creating an "us and them" mentality. Today the "them" are illegal immigrants. Tomorrow it will be all immigrants and all people of color or non-Christians."

"That is mixing up the heifer with the herd. Americans are not like that."

"I hope not," Deliah said in her clipped British accent. "People said Germans were not like that too, and yet they followed Hitler's plan to cleanse Europe of 'sub-humans'."

"Sub-humans?" Tex had never heard this word before.

"In the Nazi world, that is everyone who is not white."

Tex remembered a story Audrey had told him about her grandmother who was in the French Resistance fighting the Nazis. Now Audrey was in the middle of the Dik Dik camp, doing the same thing.

He was feeling useless, and Deliah acted like he was one step away from becoming a neo-Nazi. He didn't understand why this was happening. He had been the best of the recruits during training. So why did he feel like he was trying to put socks on a rooster?

Day 7. 11:00 pm, Middle-of-Nowhere, Colorado

The delivery truck pulled to a stop in front of the warehouse. The truck was once white, but now road and snow debris blanketed the sides. Grime plastered both license plates, making them unreadable. The driver honked his horn once, a short bleep more than a full get-out-of-my-way blast. Seconds later, ten men were unloading wooden crates from the truck. In seven minutes, the truck, now empty, pulled away from the warehouse. No one except the men inside saw the delivery take place.

㉒

Secret Passages

Day 8. 10:30 am, White House, Washington DC

When Marshall Cox hadn't showed up for work on Monday morning, Lee started to worry. He wasn't really sure why. Not because he finally had his prank ready, or because he missed being ribbed every day by a guy who thought he was better than everyone else. But in a way, it had become quite expected and part of the order of the day. Lee knew from years at school that once the pecking order was established, there was no changing it. You just found a way to live with it. He figured Marshall's life was probably no cakewalk either.

The photo download from his tie clip camera had barely finished when Ria burst into the room. She had been out on rounds, delivering intelligence reports.

"Hey, did you see Marshall while you were out?" Lee asked.

"No."

"Do you remember seeing him on Friday or over the weekend?"

"No." A smile crept across her face.

"Don't you think that's a little odd?"

"Like I care," Ria said.

"I'm just saying, for a guy who normally has his nose in everybody's business, he seems awfully quiet. Remember, CONTROL told us to keep our eyes open to anything unusual."

"Unusual? That would be Marshall every day. You can search for him. I've got work to do."

Lee saved the folder with the downloaded pictures, naming it "General Research" in the hopes that if Ria did any snooping on his computer, the file wouldn't spark her interest. After the incident with the dead drop, he didn't need to give her any more reasons to doubt his ability as a spy.

Lee would look for Marshall. A small beacon tracker was in a box of equipment he was supposed to return to the Intel Center. The last time he had seen Marshall was when he put Lee's tracking beacon in his pocket. Lee had been certain at the time that Marshall did it just to ruin his experiment. But now Lee could experiment on Marshall instead. When he found Marshall, the joke would be on him.

Ria was completely focused on her e-mails as Lee slid the beacon tracker into his pocket. He headed straight for the Secret Service office. The door to Crenshaw's office was closed, but Mrs. Werner was at her post.

"Hi, Mrs. Werner."

"Hi, hon. What can I do for you?"

Mrs. Werner was always nice to both Lee and Ria during their long waits outside Crenshaw's office. She was very organized and everyone seemed to gravitate to her when they had a problem or needed to get something done. Lee suspected that Mrs. Werner was more in charge than Crenshaw.

"Have you seen Marshall?"

"No. But if you happen to spot him, please tell him Mr. Crenshaw has been looking for him."

"How long has he been looking for him?"

"Since Friday. He never finished an assignment. Marshall is usually so good about checking in. He must be at one of the Intern Orientation programs."

"Thanks Mrs. Werner, I'll let you know if I see him."

Lee headed down the hall to the Mail Room, stopping two security guards and several staffers. No one could remember seeing Marshall during the last few days. He continued down the hall to the Library. Since Crenshaw was looking for Marshall, he could use that as his excuse if he got caught. A quick check up and down the corridor, and Lee slipped inside.

This was the room where less formal private meetings took place. Lee tried to imagine what had gone on in here the day he had splattered the white tea roses with one of his pen experiments gone wrong. The room was painted a cheerful yellow with red and yellow striped curtains along the windows. The shelves were packed with volumes on history, mostly about the White House, former presidents and past wars. Lee noticed there were no books for kids, or much on science.

Lee set the tracker on a table and turned it on. He punched in the frequency of the beacon that Marshall had filched. To his surprise, the tracker lit up showing a strong signal. The beacon was close. Really close.

Lee walked six paces until he came to the wall. The tracker indicated the beacon was directly below him. He was about to go back downstairs, when a small handle on the wall caught his eye. There was a door. Not a normal door, but one that had been cleverly designed to match the paneling. He grasped the handle and tugged. With a click, it opened.

The staircase curved down and around along the wall of the building. It was not very long and ended in a small room with several doors. The room had a table with a few chairs around it. A case of bottled water was shoved in the corner. Lee watched the tracker strobe quicken. He had to be really close. Opening one of the doors he found a bench, a mirror, and a few hooks on the wall. It looked like a dressing room. He tried the handle on the second door, but it wouldn't budge. The tracker emitted a solid red light. He heard something—kind of like a low moan.

"Anybody in there?" Lee said. He heard something strike the door.

"I said, is anybody in there?" Lee pressed his ear to the door. He heard the thump again. He was pretty sure it was someone thumping, and not the furnace or some other antiquated piece of mechanical equipment that hid in the basement. He squatted down, eye level with the door handle. There was no keyhole, but something was jammed between the molding and the door, causing the door to stick.

Lee pulled out his pen and began wiggling and jiggling it up and down the inside of the doorjamb. Part way up, he struck something. A lapel pin popped out. Lee shoved it into his pocket and pulled the door open. There, bound and gagged on the floor, was Marshall Cox.

Day 8. 10:30 am, Austin, Texas

"Welcome to Talking about Books," the radio announcer's familiar voice blasted across the airwaves. The program, not just popular in Texas, but across the U.S., featured interviews with authors of the hottest new books. Appearing on Talking about Books was a sure way to make the best seller's list.

"Today I have Susan Kaine in the studio to talk about her new book, *Ten Steps to a Greater America*. Welcome, Susan."

"Thank you," a woman responded. "Thank you for letting me share my views about how to make American strong again." Her voice rang with confidence. She had a plan to improve the economy, create jobs for workers, and deliver on the American dream. Her voice said it all.

The host poured on the praise. "Everyone is talking about the ten steps, which seem very simple. For example, you call for a change in U.S. immigration policy, so foreigners don't take American jobs or live off taxpayer money..."

23

Seeing Stars

Day 8. 10:30 am, Dik Dik Reserve, Tanzania

The Range Master separated the recruits into groups of five. Audrey was assigned with Freda and three others. Today's lesson covered hand grenades. Audrey focused on everything the Range Master said, particularly the 'you have ten seconds after pulling the pin to throw the grenade' part. The first time she pulled the safety and started the countdown from ten, she got mixed up and forgot where she was. The Range Master hollered at her until her ears rang. After that, she said a rhyme about a mouse and a clock so her mind wouldn't wander to the 'what ifs.' She had to make sure she tossed the grenade long before the last Hickory Dickory Dock.

They were to duck behind the stacked sandbags after the throw. A couple of tosses later, Audrey was thinking it was all pretty simple.

That was just before a green orb landed between her and Freda. Someone screamed. Audrey leapt without thinking. It was part arabesque, part tackle. She flew at Freda, knocking her backwards. They tumbled over one another before landing safely on the far side of the sandbag barrier. Audrey hit her head hard against Freda's. First there were stars and then an excruciating pain in her ears. The world went silent and then black.

When Audrey came to, the ringing in her ears made her want to vomit. It was dark. She could hear someone whimpering. She felt the slick nylon of her sleeping bag. As her eyes adjusted, she realized she was in a tent, her tent. The sounds were coming from Freda. Audrey moved to sit up. Her head pounded with each beat of her heart, and her ears felt on fire. She crawled towards Freda.

"Are you okay?" Audrey asked.

"Yes," Freda said between sobs.

"Are you hurt?"

"You wouldn't understand. Go away."

Audrey drew closer. She could see a large bandage on Freda's left arm. "Does it hurt a lot?"

"Just a little. A rock cut my arm." Freda covered her eyes with her hands and sobbed.

Audrey reached for her hand. She saw a mixture of pain and terror in Freda's eyes. "You saved my life," Freda whispered, choking on the last word.

"Did I? I don't really remember. It happened so fast. Is everyone okay?"

Freda remained silent. Audrey held her hand and waited. As much as she despised Freda for her beliefs, she hated watching her suffer. Freda no longer looked invincible. Maybe she could finally get some information.

"Why are you here?" Audrey asked.

"I'm so afraid. I don't want to die."

"Then why don't you go home?"

"I can't." Freda sounded desperate.

"Why not?"

"Frederick won't let me."

"What's he going to do? Tie you to the tent? Just tell him you're out of here and hitch a ride into town."

"You don't understand. I can't."

Audrey willed herself to ignore her aching head. "Make me understand."

"If I leave, the Leader will hold Frederick responsible and punish him."

"So?"

Freda turned her head away and stared into the darkness. Audrey held her hand firmly and could feel the quaking increase. "Talk to me. Maybe I can help."

"Frederick is my brother."

Audrey caught her breath. She had never even considered this possibility. "Uh, I thought Frederick's position was important."

Freda laughed bitterly. "The Leader doesn't care about people, just followers. He rewards those who are loyal and punishes those who fail him. If I leave, the Leader will think that Frederick is not to be trusted."

Audrey was confused. She needed to find a way to make Freda open up to her. "There will be other chances for Frederick to show the Leader how loyal he is."

"This is his big chance. It's not a practice run. Frederick is responsible for all the training for Operation Eagle's Nest. After we finish here, we deploy. There are no second chances."

Freda pulled her hand away and turned her back on Audrey, her body heaving with silent sobs. "I knew you wouldn't understand."

"Freda—"

"Nothing scares you. Even when you have a hard time, you keep going. No wonder they chose you."

"Freda, I'm scared too. I don't understand what's going on. Tell me about Operation Eagles Nest."

"You don't know?" Freda turned and looked at her. Audrey shook her head.

"I can understand why they didn't tell me, but I thought for sure you, the American, would know, since you are the contact, and the operation takes place in the U.S."

Audrey felt faint. She had said the wrong thing and exposed herself. She focused all her senses on Freda. There was no choice now but go for broke. "Do you believe the Leader is doing the right thing?

Freda was silent.

If she didn't understand what motivated Freda, she would never know if she could trust her. "Is it worth dying for?"

The 'no' was almost inaudible. Audrey felt the answer more than she heard it.

"Do you want me to help you get out?"

"But Frederick—"

"We can help him, too. If we work together, we can stop this now."

Freda shut her eyes. Moments passed and her breathing softened. "What do you want me to do?"

"Tell me what you know about the Leader."

Day 8. 11:00 am, FBI HQ, Washington DC

The FBI agent rubbed his eyes as he set down the report. Cause of Death: Anthrax Poisoning.

Who would want to kill Lt. General Frank Watt? Obviously, it was someone who knew how to make the fine powder without getting killed in the process. But why?

㉔

Puzzle Pieces

Day 8. 11:00 am, White House, Washington DC

Lee fell to his knees and grabbed Marshall's wrist. There was a pulse.

"Sweet Einstein. Are you okay?"

He began releasing the tape over Marshall's mouth and around his wrists and ankles. The boy in front of him was no longer cocky and sure but really scared.

"T-T-Thanks," Marshall said, rubbing his arms to get the blood flowing. Lee helped him up and pulled out a chair. Lee took a seat across from him, ready to catch Marshall if he toppled over.

"What happened?"

"I'm not sure," Marshall said. "I went to the Mail Room

to do some copying for Crenshaw, and the next thing I knew I was down here."

"When was that?" Lee asked.

"In the afternoon."

"I mean what day?"

"Friday. What's today?"

"Monday." Lee looked carefully at Marshall. Three days was a long time without food and water. Lee grabbed a bottle of water from one of the cases on the floor.

"Do you have any reason for anyone to be angry with you?"

"No, everyone likes me or at least pretends to…on account of Grandpa and Dad."

Lee raised his eyebrows.

"You sure ask a lot of questions. Are you planning on being an interrogator when you grow up?" Marshall scowled at him. The water dribbling down his chin gave him the look of a drooling baby.

Lee leaned back and cleaned his glasses on his shirt. "Sorry, I just like understanding the logic behind everything. It seems odd that someone would go to all this trouble without a good reason. Besides, how would anyone know about this place? It's the staircase to nowhere."

"Actually, this is where all the performers at the White House get ready. If there had been a dinner with music, I would have been discovered. It just so happens, nothing is scheduled for a week." Marshall wiped his chin with his sleeve and tried to stand up. Lee caught him when he teetered and guided him back into the chair.

"So is there another way out of here?" Lee asked.

"No, you have to go out the way you came in."

"Someone's not going to be very happy when they see you in the halls again, so I think we should figure out what you might have heard or seen that would have gotten you sent down here."

"I was making copies when a fax came in for Crenshaw," Marshall said. "I picked the fax up," Marshall paused. "That's the last thing I remember."

Marshall's color was coming back, but he really didn't look very good. Lee found a smashed candy bar wedged in his pocket.

"It's not much." Lee handed the candy to Marshall. "You're probably pretty hungry right now." Lee pushed the lapel pin deeper into his pocket.

Marshall shoved the candy in whole and began chomping loudly.

"Now let's get you out of here," Lee said. Holding Marshall steady, they headed up the stairs.

At the outer door, Lee paused a moment, listening, before opening it just a crack. The Library was empty. Lee stuck his head out into the hallway, and for the moment it was quiet too.

"Go home," Lee said. "Don't go back to your desk or get your coat or anything. Don't come to work tomorrow or the next day. Better yet, don't come until I call you. I'll fix it with Crenshaw."

"But what if somebody needs me?"

"Somebody just tried to kill you, Marshall. Don't you get it?"

Marshall's chin dropped. Without another word, he walked out of the Library. Lee waited thirty seconds before leaving and went in the opposite direction. Everyone coming to the White House had to sign in and out. Would anyone notice that Marshall Cox was signing out for the first time in three days?

Lee burst into his office and began taping blank sheets of paper to the wall.

"Where have you been?" Ria asked.

"I found Marshall. Something's going on. Help me find the pattern."

"What?"

Lee drew a circle on the wall and labeled it "Marshall Cox." He drew a second circle overlapping the first and wrote "Fax." He drew a third circle, not touching the first two and wrote "Dead Capitol Police Chief."

Ria grabbed a marker and added two circles: "Freedom Federation" and "Stolen Weapons," each overlapping a third larger circle labeled "Montana."

On a fresh piece of paper, Lee put Todd Geringer's name in a circle and wrote down "suspicious." Studying the Venn diagram the circles had formed, he wondered where Todd's circle should go in relation to the others.

Paper in hand, he froze. "I totally forgot." Lee slid into his chair and opened the file named General Research.

"What are you talking about?" Ria asked, eyes focused on the expanding diagram.

"I went to Todd Geringer's office to get my spy pen back,

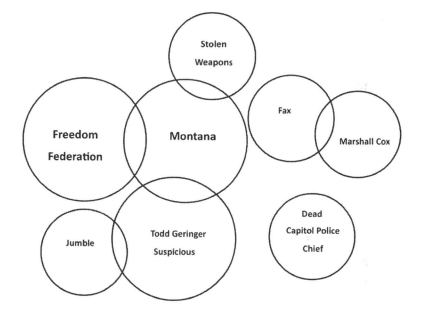

Stolen
Weapons

Freedom
Federation

Montana

Fax

Marshall Cox

Jumble

Todd Geringer
Suspicious

Dead
Capitol Police
Chief

Venn Diagram

and I found out Todd kept a file on Montana."

Ria rolled her chair next to Lee. "What spy pen?" she asked, looking over his shoulder at the images in the file.

"How'd you get these?"

Lee didn't answer, but focused on the images. There were documents on the vice president's schedule for a fundraising trip to Montana, a list of campaign donations from people in Montana, and lots of policy documents on health care, social security, and the environment. The last photos were of newspaper clippings of the new Jumble. One of the puzzles had a handwritten note: True Americans Must Stand Together to Purify and Save the Nation.

A knot was growing in Lee's stomach and for once he knew it was not food related. Why would Todd keep this Jumble in a file named Montana?

Day 8. 11:00 pm, Middle-of-Nowhere, Colorado

The men in the warehouse pried the top of the wooden crates open. Even though they were strong, it took several forceful blows with a crowbar before the nails gave way. They did not check the contents of the crates. Their orders were clear: wait for the contact from Montana. He would check each AK-47 assault rifle before they test fired them—unseen and unheard—on the range they just finished building inside the warehouse. They would test the grenades outside in a remote valley, where the sound would not travel.

As for the mountain gear, they would just have to trust the supplier who had no name or address.

㉕

Set Up

Day 9. 10:30 am, Mt. Kilimanjaro, Tanzania

At daybreak, the recruits started the climb to 15,000 feet. The route zigzagged up and down, to help them get used to the altitude. The hiking poles clicking against the rocks sounded more like a swarm of crickets than an army training for an as-of-yet unknown assault. Going down turned out to be the hard part. After six hours of trekking, Audrey's legs trembled.

"Why do we have to carry all this stuff?" Audrey said, leaning heavily on her poles.

"Fredrick says in the actual operation, we'll have to carry heavy loads." Freda dropped her voice at the mention of her brother.

"Has he said anything more about the target?"

Freda frowned. "Only that the Leader chose this location because of the altitude."

"The altitude?" Mt. Kilimanjaro was 19,000-some-thing feet tall. "There are other mountains this high or higher in the Alps. Why come to Africa?"

"I don't think it's just the altitude, but the change in altitude," Freda murmured. "The final climb takes place in one day."

"I don't understand," Audrey said.

"Well, it's not a technical climb, like Everest, where you need all this specialized gear."

"So the target is someplace high we can walk up—no snow or ice?"

"I didn't say that," Freda responded sharply. "I know we will be working with rock climbing gear, ice clamps, and picks next."

"How do you know?"

"Fredrick was going through the gear last night. Tomorrow we head for the snow fields."

"To the top?" Audrey looked towards the peak of Kilimanjaro. There were actually two peaks, one higher than the other. Both seemed a bazillion miles away, reminding her of how badly her legs ached. Both peaks were covered in snow, which was odd, considering it was sunny and dry where they stood.

"I'll notify my friends. They're meeting at 8:00 tonight at the Kili Café in Moshe. Maybe they'll have some information on what the Leader is planning." Audrey spoke casually and hoped the sudden dump of information did not sound too obvious.

Freda grunted and picked up speed. Their tent was in sight. Setting up their new camp, they had chosen a patch between the rocks that gave them a good view of the mountain and was close to the open-slatted hole in the ground that was their toilet. The boys had other options, such as peeing behind the tents after dark. But when you were a girl, well, you wanted a bathroom, even if it truly was just a pit.

Audrey headed to the outhouse. It was as deluxe as the one in the first camp, only it was built on a downhill incline. That made going to the bathroom a real challenge. She had seen a number of recruits coming out, wiping their boots in the dirt. Audrey needed to get a message to the team.

Somehow, Audrey imagined her life as a spy as being slightly more elegant than hiding out in stinky outhouses. But at least she couldn't smell herself. To think that she had been worried about forgetting her face soap and how the hair color made her look so ugly! Nobody here would notice anything but the stench coming off her.

Audrey quickly entered in her password sequence and began tapping out a message to MOLECHECK.

Checking in. I'm ok. Tired.
Intel: Freda says Leader said target is high altitude mt w snow/ice.

Ops: Test set up for 2night. Advise if u c surveillance. If none, should we trust Freda? I feel uncertain.

Admin: Will check in at 6 tonight and 5 in morning. Need to know about Freda before tomorrow night when we head to the summit.

Audrey sent the message. She would know in just a few hours if Freda was really on their side.

Pounding on the outhouse door startled Audrey. Fumbling, she felt the compact slip through her fingers. She grabbed at it, but it was too late. The compact fell into the pit. Audrey stifled a scream of panic.

"There's a line out here. Hurry up!" said a chorus of voices.

Audrey adjusted her clothes as she exited. "Sorry," she mumbled. Audrey spotted Frederick leaning against a rock, watching her.

She hadn't noticed him earlier. She wondered just how much he could see through the cracks in the wooden slats. Would the glow of LCD light be noticeable? The image of him skimming through the cesspool looking for what she dropped flashed in her mind. It made her smile, but only for a heartbeat. There was no way she could ever face MOLECHECK and the other Junior Spies and admit that a toilet ate her top-secret spy equipment. She had lost her only link to the outside world.

Day 9. Morning, Across the USA

The Letter to the Editor appeared in 56 newspapers that morning. It was actually letters, because a different self-described patriotic American signed each one. Each letter differed in the number of words and the opening. Some started with Dear Sirs. Others were Dear all True Americans. The message, however, was the same. Throw out the immigrants. They were destroying America, taking away American jobs, living off the American taxpayer and ruining the moral values of good American kids.

26

Making Friends

Day 9. 10:30 am, White House, Washington DC

There were times Lee decided that being a spy was really more trouble than it was worth. It required being an extrovert, which Lee was not, and the ability to easily make friends. Ria was a natural. Maybe she was a little annoying, but as she traveled the halls on errands for Crenshaw, she always had a joke or a piece of juicy White House gossip to pass along. Everybody loved her.

The discovery yesterday of Marshall and the documents from Todd's office just complicated the puzzle. The more he studied the growing pile of evidence, the weirder his theories became. There was a picture of a check with lots of zeros from a guy with a fancy name that Lee didn't recognize. It was stapled to a copy of a newspaper article dated two days later about Senate legislation regarding money for schools which passed by only one vote–the tie break from the vice president.

Was someone trying to buy the vice president? Or were they blackmailing him? Or Todd? Lee was stumped. He felt like a lab rat being led down a series of dead-end mazes, only to be trapped in a corner, smelling cheese hidden close by. He decided it was time to go searching for a new set of clues and maybe a few cold, hard facts.

His first stop was the Mail Room. He stood over the fax machine, staring at the buttons and wondering if there was a way to pull a second copy of a document from memory. A total lack of office skills was holding him back.

"Can I help you?"

One of the president's aides was actually talking to him. She tipped her head slightly, her straight hair falling in a perfect line from her navy headband. Everything about her was perfect. Lee knew what he had to do. He was going to make a new best friend. He tipped his head in the same direction as the girl's and smiled.

"I need help with something."

"Obviously. What's up?" Her hand was now on her hip.

Lee placed his hand on his hip and tipped his butt out and tried to look casual. What he hadn't noticed was her weight was balanced on one leg, the other out slightly in front of her, giving her a casual, relaxed look. With both his feet still firmly in the same place, he looked like a concrete pillar trying to relax.

"I work for Crenshaw," he said, lowering his voice.

"No wonder you look so uncomfortable." She shifted her weight to the other foot. Lee swung his hips like a hula dancer in traction trying to mimic her move and fell into the fax machine.

"I misplaced a fax yesterday, and I was wondering if there was a way to print another one from memory?"

"It depends," she said. "Incoming faxes only go into memory if there is a paper jam or the ink is out. Otherwise, only the date and time received is stored."

"Oh." He stared at her. Say something his brain screamed; keep the conversation going. But nothing was coming out.

"Look, tell me what day the fax came through, and I'll see what I can do."

"That would be great. You can't imagine what Crenshaw can be like when you've screwed up."

"I think I have a pretty good idea." Then she smiled at Lee. "So what day did the fax come through?"

"Friday."

She pushed a few buttons. "Looks like there was just one." She hit the print button, and the fax slid out the side. Lee scooped it up and shoved it into the middle of his folder.

"Thanks for your help."

"Any time, cutie."

Lee floated out of the copy room and into the hallway. He was off to make another friend, but this time he'd remember to ask her name.

It was an hour later when he made it back to the basement office. He had acquired a box of chocolates, a tip on which team was a sure bet to win tomorrow night's playoff, and picked up a few extra bits of gossip to share with Ria. So it was disappointing when she wasn't there. He plopped into his chair and stared at the growing wall of notations, suspects, and theories. Then he remembered the folder.

The fax was addressed to Crenshaw, alerting him to a new case in Montana revolving around three young men, one with a Nazi tattoo traveling on false passports to Tanzania. They died in a car crash and never made it to Africa. A handwritten note was at the bottom.

Thought you might be interested this, given your questions on militia activity.

Marshall had stumbled onto something important. Lee grabbed a marker, making swift changes to the Venn diagram on the wall. The "Fax" circle now overlapped the "Marshall Cox" circle and the "Montana" circle. He added a new circle labeled "Deaths," overlapping "Montana," "Fax," and "Capitol Police Chief" and a second new circle, "Crenshaw," connecting to "Marshall Cox" and "Fax." The connections were growing, but he still didn't see their significance.

There had to be a key.

Day 9. 10:30 am, New York City, New York

The black limo pulled to a stop at the corner of Wall and Broad Streets. The chauffeur opened the passenger door. From the shadows of a building, a man in a navy suit and matching wool coat emerged. His expensive Swiss watch and his dollar cuff links hinted at his power in the banking world.

"Barry, I don't like meeting like this," the banker said.

"Nor I. However, it's safer than using the phone."

"Maybe, but let's keep it short. Tuesday, I'm going to cut interest rates by a full percent."

"What? Tomorrow? Couldn't you give me more notice?"

"No. So you better do your currency buys and sells today or first thing tomorrow morning."

The Chairman of the Federal Reserve didn't wait for the chauffer to open the door. He was gone as quickly as he came, leaving Barry VanderCourt alone to plan how he would turn $10 million dollars into $20 million by playing the currency markets with insider knowledge. Funding a revolution required a lot of money.

㉗
Ops Test

Day 9. 7:30 pm, Moshi, Tanzania

According to the ops plan, Tex and Deliah returned to the café at nightfall to set the trap. Audrey had let it slip to Freda that she had friends in Moshe, ready to help, who would be meeting in the café at 8:00. If Freda was trustworthy, Tex would have a boring evening on his hands. If Freda passed along the information to her Nazi friends, things could get real interesting.

Deliah watched the front entrance to the café from across the street, while Tex sat at a table near the back where he could see the kitchen, the back door, and the view through the front window. MOLECHECK's instructions were clear. Watch for anyone loitering in the café or outside. Or anyone who might be taking pictures.

This was the first real spy work for Tex since he arrived, and he was determined to spot surveillance. Tex would show DEAL-MAKER he was not sympathetic to the Nazi cause. Nor was he afraid of them. If it got ugly, he would be as tough as stewed skunk. As the minutes ticked by, he daydreamed to kill the time, first taking on one bad guy and then another, and then the whole team, with him the only cowboy left standing.

No one came in; no one left. He was alone with two waiters, a cook, and a bartender who kept pestering him to order more food. Moshi did not have much of a nightlife.

An hour passed before shadows outside the front window caught his attention. Deliah was talking to a man. Tex could not see the details of his face, but made out the profile of a crooked nose. Tex had seen that face somewhere before. Where?

"Excuse me, mind if I join you?" Tex turned to see a girl dressed in hiking clothes. When did she come in?

"I'm getting ready to leave," Tex said, eyes back on the man with Deliah.

"Well, maybe you could sit with me for a few minutes. I get terrible service when I eat alone."

Tex turned back to the girl. She was smiling, her hand resting on the chair. Tex smiled back. His mom always had the same complaint back home.

"Sure, have a seat and get your order in. But I'm going to have to leave in a few minutes." Deliah was still with the man. Tex racked his brain for a connection. He wore western clothes, but not the hiking kind.

"You waiting for friends?" the girl asked.

Tex brought his attention back to the table. "Yeah."

"I'm Helga," she said.

"Tex."

"Like Texas? You are an American?"

"Just Tex, but I'm from Texas." An image of his bus ride from the airport to Moshi flashed through his memory. He looked back outside. Was that the same man from the bus?

"And your friends, also from Texas?"

"Ah, no." Tex said without thinking.

"Maybe Colorado? I hear there are big mountains in Colorado."

The hairs on the back of Tex's neck tingled. He looked more intently at this girl. Why mention Colorado?

"Where are you from?" Tex asked. "Your English is good, but you have that big city talk."

Helga laughed. "I'm from Austria, but not from the city. We have more goats than people where I come from." She paused for a breath and continued. "And your friends, city or country people?"

Tex stood and waved to the waiter. "Can we have a menu over here?" Turning to the girl, he said, "Thanks for the howdy, but I gotta go." While giving her a salute with one hand, he pressed on the hidden latch of his silver belt buckle and snapped a picture of the girl before heading for the door.

Deliah caught his eye and abruptly ended the conversation with the mysterious man, who walked off just fast enough to make Tex suspicious.

"Who was that?" Tex said.

"A tourist," Deliah's face was flushed. Tex sensed she was worried.

"A tourist watching the café?"

"No. Just asking for directions."

"See anything inside?" Deliah asked.

"Nope, but I have an odd feeling about that man," Tex said. "You've seen him before?"

"He's just a tourist, Tex. Stop seeing ghosts."

"That was no ghost," Tex said through clinched teeth. "I've seen him before. I think he was on the bus with Audrey and me when we arrived in Moshi."

"Yes, the tourist bus. Who was the girl?" Deliah shot back.

"Wash off your war paint, Deliah. She's an Austrian. Said her name was Helga."

"What did she want?"

"Didn't want to sit alone because waiters ignored her."

Deliah's eyebrows shot up. "Maybe in the U.S., but not in Moshi. What did she say?"

Tex replayed their conversation and when he came to the Colorado part, he stopped. Audrey's cover story is that she's from Colorado Springs.

Tex looked back at the café. The girl was gone. Why hadn't he figured it out sooner? He felt dumb as a prairie dog. "I got her picture. We can send it to Audrey to see if she can identify her."

"No we can't," Deliah said.

"We can't stand here whistling up the wind. That girl was

121

here checking me out. Audrey needs to know."

"MIND-READER missed her 5 o'clock check-in time."

"How do you know that?" Tex asked, startled.

"MOLECHECK just sent me a message."

"So she's late. Don't get your tail up. She'll check in when she can. She's not the type to go solo." Tex tried to sound cool, but it irked him that MOLECHECK was telling Deliah things without also telling Tex.

"MOLECHECK says her commo equipment has failed. The signal is dead. Either she broke it or someone broke it for her."

Tex's heart skipped a beat. "Then how are we going to warn her about Freda?"

"Someone will need to make contact with her on the mountain."

Tex stood up straight. Now that was more like it. "Like us."

"Yes, but—"

"Is her beacon on?"

"Yes, but—"

"Well, what are we waiting for?" Tex said. He was not going to leave Audrey stranded. Freda had just double- crossed his girl.

"We need a climbing permit to even get on the mountain, and none is available."

Tex tensed. Rules had never stopped him before. "Who says we're gonna climb?"

Day 9. 10:00 pm, Dar es Salaam, Tanzania

The night duty park ranger rubbed his eyes and tried to ignore the ringing phone. Would they never give up? He had told them three times all the climbing permits for Kilimanjaro had been sold. The next available permits were next season and there were no exceptions. It was a matter of safety.

㉘ Poem Code

Day 10. 7:30 am, Georgetown, Washington DC

Ria flopped on the bed and opened her e-mail. There were dozens of new messages, all from the Freedom Federation.

There was movement in the hallway. Mrs. Edencamp?

"Ria?" She could hear Lee's muffled voice. "Ready to go?"

"I'll meet you downstairs," Ria said as she shoved her laptop into her backpack. Mrs. Edencamp was busy in the front sitting room setting a table for a formal etiquette class. Ria was glad to have a work excuse to miss these afternoon torture sessions.

They exited the Farragut Square metro stop fifteen minutes later. Ria was feeling grumpy. She had found out from Lee, who heard it from the Intel Center grapevine, that Tex and Audrey had been sent to Tanzania, Africa. The boys with the tattoos and fake passports were going to Tanzania, too. Why didn't she get to go?

Her fit of jealousy eased slightly as she and Lee walked past the lines of tourists waiting for the first White House tour of the day. She flashed her badge to the security detail in the guard house and walked right in. She loved her hard little badge with the red 'A.' To her, it was more valuable than the most expensive piece of jewelry.

Once at their desks in their basement office, Ria began to read the rest of the Freedom Federation messages.

"Lee," she said in a throaty whisper, "Look at this." He rolled his chair beside her as e-mails continued to scroll. This was no longer about barbecues in Montana. Something big was getting ready to happen. This was a call to arms, a gathering of the troops.

"Where did you get these?" Lee asked.

"I joined the Freedom Federation."

"They didn't care that you're a kid?"

"It's not like they asked a lot of questions," Ria said. "I just had to declare loyalty to the cause."

A pattern was starting to emerge. The headings began with "Dear Concerned Citizen," and then moved to "Time is Running Out" to "A Threat to our 2nd Amendment Rights." At first it was nothing more than disgruntled rants. It just seemed odd to Ria that there were so many e-mails in a two-day time period. What was the point of sending the same thing over and over?

"Let's do a computerized word-for-word comparison to

find repeated words or phrases," Lee said.

Every message contained the same eleven words, not in the same sentence, but hidden in plain sight in each text. True Americans Must Stand Together to Purify and Save the Nation. "That's familiar," Ria said.

"Yes, it is." Lee scooted his chair to the wall full of taped paper covered with circles. He pointed to Todd Geringer. "In his files there were some Jumbles torn from the newspaper. Those same words were handwritten on one of them."

"What if it's a code?"

"You mean like a letter substitution code?"

Ria sat up straight and looked at Lee.

"Like a poem code. It could be a key to a code."

Ria grabbed a pencil and drew a grid. Poem codes only looked complicated. The name came from the practice of using a poem as the key, but any phrase could be used as long as it had enough words and was easy to memorize. Only five words would be used from the poem to serve as the key. The first challenge was to figure out which five words. "Give me today's Jumble," Ria said. Lee handed over the newspaper.

ACGIJ   AOJSK   FORMO   CXSID   NSNIM
HTPKA   JEGTO   SLGSH   CSFAA   VQNNI
PBWOU   PTDYI   QLAGB   UEZRS

It wasn't like the normal Jumble. This one had way too many words. Ria looked at the first group of letters: ACGIJ. This would tell her the five words.

She hoped that whoever wrote the code kept it simple. A is the first letter of the alphabet, so she selected the first word of the key: TRUE. C is the third letter, meaning the third word of the poem: MUST. Using the same system, she selected PURIFY SAVE and THE as the remaining key. Now, it was a matter of substituting letters for numbers.

They worked long past lunch as Lee's stomach growled. Lee didn't complain once, but kept running his hands through his spiky hair, checking her work. He caught several mistakes as she substituted the key letters for numbers,

"OMG." The pencil scratches stopped. "It works." Ria handed Lee the paper. The day's Jumble had been transformed from letters to words. The meaning was unmistakable:

POTUS ASSASSINATION GO

"Do you think this is real or just some odd coincidence? Can POTUS stand for anything other than the President of the United States?" Ria asked.

Lee checked the work one more time. "Someone else is supposed to figure it out. That's why the message was put in the form of a puzzle that could go into hundreds of papers across the country."

"Todd had the Jumble hidden in his files. If he's in on it, who else is?" Ria said, staring at the circles on the wall.

Lee removed his glasses, cleaned them with his shirttail, and replaced them. "We need to change the circle with the Jumble so that it overlaps with the Freedom—"

"That's it," Ria said, cutting Lee off. Bounding to the wall, she drew one large circle around all the circles. "This is the link, the Freedom Federation."

"We need to alert Crenshaw," Lee said. "And we have to be

really careful about who sees this."

Ria hoped they were really off track. Otherwise, the worst was getting ready to happen.

Day 10. 7:30 am, Undisclosed Location, USA

The Leader's phone vibrated five times.

"Yes?"

"Your delivery has been inventoried. The goods are in proper condition," Barry VanderCourt said.

"You had doubts?"

"None."

"Well, perhaps you should."

VanderCourt's only response was a growl.

"The recruit you sent may be untrustworthy," the Leader said, voice hard as steel.

"What do you mean? Which recruit?"

"The girl."

"I didn't send any girls. I sent three men. My best."

"Then, my friend, we have a bigger problem."

㉙
Soaring

Day 10. 1:00 pm, Mt. Kilimanjaro, Tanzania

Tex's feet pounded the earth, picking up speed despite the heavy load. He could hear Deliah breathing hard through the intercom, but she remained shoulder-to-shoulder with him. He willed himself to go faster before the ground disappeared. There was a tug on the harness at five steps and then the pull at three. They weren't heading down, but lifting up as the wing of the glider found the currents. Tex pulled back on the control bar, and the glider soared.

"Wheeeee," Deliah squealed.

Tex grinned. Maybe she really was human after all. When he suggested gliding onto the mountain as the fastest way to get to Audrey, Deliah found him a state-of-the-art glider right away. The owner of the adventure travel store didn't ask any questions once he checked Tex out with a short solo flight. It didn't hurt that the owner knew Deliah's father.

Tex leaned to his left, bringing the glider around. Before taking off, he had an in-depth briefing on the thermals and currents around the mountain. Staying up didn't sound like it would be a problem. The owner's only caution was on the northeast side of Kilimanjaro, where the crosswinds could be too turbulent.

"Activate the GPS," Tex said into the microphone attached to his helmet.

"Done. I'm working on our course," Deliah said.

The glider was a tandem, with two harnesses side by side. He could see the LCD screen of the Global Positioning device. "Have you picked up Audrey's signal yet?"

"No, but according to the geocoords MOLECHECK gave us, we won't be able to pick her up signal until we reach the saddle of the Loikoktok side of the mountain."

Tex surveyed the scenery below. They were flying over the rain forest, which spread across the lowest zone of Kilimanjaro. The canopy from the trees completely blocked any view of the ground. "Wow, it looks like a velvet green carpet."

"Yeah, it looks completely different from up here," Deliah said.

"How many times have you climbed Kili?" Tex asked, feeling a twinge of jealousy.

"I've been in the rain forest many times with my dad, and up to a few of the lower camps."

"And up top?"

"Never."

Ahead of them, a hawk stretched its wings and soared upward. Tex leaned slightly to his right, directing the glider to follow the bird. When Tex felt the thermal, he pulled up his wing, and caught the stream of warm air and altitude.

As the hours flew by, the scenery changed from green to brownish green. By late afternoon, the rocky face of the mountain dominated, like jagged brown teeth. Their altitude masked the sheerness of the mountain below.

The GPS began beeping.

"We've got her," Deliah said. The flashing dot was Audrey, or at least her boots. Before Tex and Audrey had left for Africa, MOLECHECK had implanted a miniature transmitter in each of their boots, just in case.

Tex flew towards the signal. Instead of searching for currents, he was looking for people.

"I see colors on your left," Deliah said.

The setting sun cast deep shadows on the ground making it hard to see. Tex pointed the glider down to get a better look. As the glider soared behind the ridgeline, it was buffeted by a sudden blast of air. It was like hitting a brick wall, or an invisible one. The glider pitched dangerously towards the mountain.

"Grab the bar and lean with me," Tex called out. Together they battled the wind. The glider zigzagged like a crazed hummingbird.

"We've gotta land. Look for a flat spot," Tex yelled into the mic. They were rapidly losing altitude.

Deliah pointed to a spot below. "Can we make it?"

They muscled the left wing up, sending them rushing toward what looked like a large stone mushroom. A second blast of air sent them hard to the right, as another current hit them from above. Both leaned with all their weight to the left and pulled back again on the control bar. The glider came down hard, their feet scraping the top of the mushroom rock before hitting the ground below.

"So how far off course are we?" Tex said rolling out of his harness before helping Deliah.

Deliah retrieved the GPS from her jacket pocket. "Too far to hike before sundown. I think we'd better bunk down for the night."

Tex frowned. "But we gotta get a hitch on to reach Audrey. Before it's too late."

"Hiking at night is a sure way to get ourselves killed since we're not on a trail."

"We have no choice." Tex set his jaw.

Deliah released her backpack from the glider frame. She hit the buttons of the GPS in rapid succession. "Eight miles, north, northeast. We're at 14,206 feet. We climb to 15,400 feet and the Kibo Huts." She took off in long strides, not even looking back to check for Tex.

Day 10. 5:00 pm, Kili Ranger Station, Tanzania

Ranger Amali looked through his binoculars a second time just to make sure he wasn't seeing things. He searched the sky.

It was gone.

He could have sworn he saw a glider, which was impossible. Gliders were forbidden on the mountain. Too dangerous.

No point in reporting it. He'd just get laughed at, like the time he spotted the fabled leopard, from Hemingway's *The Snows of Kilimanjaro*.

㉚

Bugging Out

Day 10. 5:00 pm, White House, Washington DC

The meeting convened in Crenshaw's office. Besides senior Secret Service detail, several key members of the president's staff attended. That left only a corner on the floor for Ria and Lee to squeeze into. Ria had forwarded a copy of the code and decryption and it was projected on the screen opposite them.

"That's some kid you got assigned to you," Agent Palanski chuckled. "Does anyone in this room remember how to break a code? And with just a pencil?" Ria's curls began standing on end. The agent had a way of saying things that made even a compliment sound like an insult.

"Now I'm the first to err on the side of caution," Crenshaw began, "But this isn't the first time we've received information about militia groups threatening the president. I recommend the president and her family be moved to Camp David immediately."

"You can't be serious." It was the president's chief of staff. Ria only saw him when he was walking with the president or in his office next to the Oval Office. "She has a full schedule of appointments and several important world leaders arriving for meetings."

"Sending the president out of DC will only alarm the American people. What do we tell them?" It was the press secretary. "Plus the VP is out of town until tomorrow."

Lee and Ria exchanged glances. They hadn't told Crenshaw about Todd yet.

"If we move her to Camp David, she can still meet with foreign leaders, but she will be surrounded by a full Marine guard and 125 acres of woods." Crenshaw rifled through his papers in search of the president's weekly schedule.

"No can do, Boss," Agent Palanski said. "Unless you want POTUS peeing in those woods."

"What?" Crenshaw snapped his head to look at Palanski.

"There's no plumbing in the Presidential Cabin."

"No plumbing? Why?" Crenshaw looked confused.

"The pipes are being replaced. Won't be any running water for a month, at least."

"What buffoon authorized this?" Crenshaw growled.

"You did," Palanski said with no hesitation.

Ria had to bite her tongue to keep from laughing. From now on, she'd call Crenshaw Special Buffoon in Charge.

Crenshaw looked like he was going to explode. The veins in his neck bulged, and he was grinding his teeth.

"How about the Rocky Retreat?" Palanski suggested.

"Does it have plumbing?" the chief of staff asked.

"It's ready. I inspected the facility a month ago," Palanski said. "It is a fortress this time of year, now that the first snows have blanketed the area."

A shadow crossed Crenshaw's face. "The retreat is close to 10,000 feet. Landing a helicopter there this time of year could be treacherous." Crenshaw's doubt was evident.

"Good. Keeps the crazies away," Palanski said. "You have a better solution?"

Crenshaw shook his head. "I want them out of here in an hour. Palanski, I leave it to you to assign the security detail."

"I'll get to work creating the story," the press secretary said, leaving the room.

Bodies moved from the office at a rapid pace. Even Crenshaw had headed down the hall, forgetting that Ria and Lee had asked for a "six-eyes" meeting.

Palanski reached down to pick up the code sheet. "Nice job, kiddies, saved me a lot of work." He gave them more of a sneer than a smile as he walked out.

Ria and Lee slumped down on the couch to wait.

"What exactly did Agent Palanski mean when he said we saved him a lot of work?" Ria said.

"Not really sure," Lee said. "But check this out. I found it in the lock when I discovered Marshall. Kind of looks like the lapel pins the Secret Service detail wears."

"Hmmm." Ria took the pin and began playing with it. "I don't think the Buffoon in Charge and Palanski like each other very much."

Lee laughed. "Maybe, but in a lab experiment, there is no such thing as a coincidence."

"Meaning?"

"It's a coincidence that Camp David is out of water?"

Ria turned Lee's question over in her mind, trying to fit it into the mental jigsaw puzzle she had constructed. "Time to contact MOLECHECK. Todd isn't the only one getting those messages. The president is flying into a trap."

Lee started to say something, but the sound of a helicopter drowned him out, blowing the leaves clinging on the trees against the window like tiny little bullets.

Day 10. 5:30pm, Missoula, Montana

Officer Bud Schultz looked up at the tap on the door and smiled. "Hi Shirley, what's up?"

"I know you're not on the case anymore, but I just got a call from a guy asking about the three dead John Doe's, you know, the boys killed in that car accident."

"Who was it?"

"Well, that's the odd thing. The guy hung up when I asked his name. But I traced the call."

"That's my girl. You're going to make a great police officer. What did you find out?"

"The call came from the Bitterroot News. It's a small, conservative paper owned by Barry VanderCourt."

"The militia supporter VanderCourt?"

"Yes, sir."

㉛
The Blues

Day 11. 1:00 am, Tanzania, Mt. Kilimanjaro,

The serpent's many eyes glowed high in the night sky. Audrey looked towards Uhuru, the peak of Kilimanjaro. The teams departed in ten-minute intervals. The assault team would go last. She and Freda stood at the bottom, watching the line of bodies, lit only by headlamps, wind across the switchbacks on their way to the summit. Audrey hopped from one foot to the other slapping her double-mittened hands. The air bit at the tops of her cheeks not covered by her balaclava, the special-issue knit hat that folded down to a face mask that made her look like a bank robber.

The pre-departure briefing had been short. Frederick unrolled a large map of Mt. Kilimanjaro. Pointing to a red line marked on the map, he showed them their route, and most importantly, revealed why they were taking it.

"This will be a more difficult ascent than in the Rockies, especially the 200-foot approach to the target."

So that was it. The target was somewhere in the Rocky Mountains. Frederick still didn't reveal what the specific target was. It could be anything. She no longer had a way to communicate with her team, but she could still capture evidence. Audrey held her flashlight over the notes and maps and photographed each one with the camera hidden in the lens.

"Fall in line," a voice said in the darkness. Audrey stepped in behind Freda, setting her hiking poles into a back and forth rhythm. "Pole-pole" is what they had heard for the last three days. At this elevation, the pole served as both a timing device for each heavy step and something to lean on when you could not go on.

For the next several hours, Audrey walked like a zombie. One pole, one foot forward, breathe. Second foot, second pole forward, breathe. Move without thinking, without feeling. She wore as much clothing as she could under the standard-issue down parka. She was still cold. Her toes no longer had any feeling. Her hands operated like claws belonging to someone else. Only two parts of her body were warm. Her thighs, which burned with each step, and her lungs, which seared with pain each time she drew a breath.

She stared at the back of Freda's head, backlit by her headlamp, and memorized the stitches of Freda's hat, just to keep her brain moving, too. She was worried about Freda.

Could she trust her? She never learned the results of the ops test. Her senses were telling her two different things, that Freda was scared and angry. But with whom she couldn't tell.

"Halt!" came a cry up ahead as the forward motion stopped. There was shouting and the sound of boots pounding down toward them. The headlamps bouncing around her made it hard to tell where anyone was headed. Two porters brushed past, carrying a body.

The narrow light cast from her headlamp momentarily lit up the threesome. Maybe it was her brain playing tricks, but the head of the hiker being carried down rolled in her direction as they passed. His face was completely blue. Blue! She wanted to scream, but there was not enough oxygen to squeeze out the sound.

Day 11. 3:00 am, Undisclosed Location, USA

The Leader's order to Frederick was short and to the point. Kill the American girl. Make it look like a climbing accident. As for the boy named Tex, the Leader ordered his capture. He would talk, sooner or later, and tell them just who they were working for.

32

Blowing Wind

Day 11. 5:00 am, Mt. Kilimanjaro, Tanzania

Tex was a hurting puppy. He and Deliah were climbing quickly to 15,000 feet with no time to acclimate. The headache was the first thing he noticed. It started at the back of his head and worked its way forward right between his eyes. He had to stop every few steps to gasp for air. And then he heard it. A long, loud honk. Then he smelled it. Rotten eggs. He was farting. Every time he took a few steps, an explosive blast passed through him.

"I'm near about past goin'," Tex yelled up to Deliah. "Wait up."

"I'm waiting," she said.

"You're halfway up the trail."

"Waiting."

"Can you come down?"

"No."

"Why not?" He heard another loud blast of air.

"That's why."

"Every time I stand up my mind sits down." A noxious cloud he couldn't walk out of fast enough surrounded him.

"This happens, you know."

"What?"

"The farting. Perfectly normal."

"Get outta here."

"In the climbing world, it's called high altitude flatus expulsion."

"You're pulling my leg."

"Outside pressure decreases and the pressure on the body increases. I don't make this stuff up."

With a loud toot, Tex scrambled after Deliah. He didn't even care about the pounding headache. He was out in nature and free to fart. A girl even told him it was okay. He was in tall cotton.

They reached the Kibo huts an hour later. The camp had already been broken down and moved. They had missed Audrey. Tex kicked through some trash, hoping to find something.

"They're heading for the summit." Deliah pointed toward a string of lights snaking up the mountain.

"So we wait for her to come back this way?"

"They will descend on the Marangu route on the other side. The Loitokitok route is only for ascent," Deliah said.

"Okay, we go after her."

"This is the most difficult and dangerous part of the climb. We won't catch up to them. We need rest and food."

Deliah studied Tex, making him feel uncomfortable.

'We will wait until sunrise and try and catch her on the downhill side." Deliah plopped down in front of a small circle of rocks and stirred the embers to get a fire going. She pulled a small tin pot and some tea from her backpack along with some cheese and bread. "You need to eat."

Tex sat next to her, his head pounding again. "Nothing for me, I feel like I'm going to be sick."

Deliah watched him. Could she hear his erratic breathing? "Drink the tea. It will help the headaches. I promise."

They drank their tea in silence. Tex's thoughts bounced back and forth between his misery and Audrey. If he didn't pull it together, he might never see her again. And if he did see her, he wouldn't be able to look her in the eye. She'd know just how big a failure he was.

The sounds of shouting in Swahili and the pounding of boots drew Tex's attention to the trailhead. Two porters and an injured hiker appeared and joined them at the fire.

Deliah knew the porters well, Prosper and Masudi. They were friends of her father. There was stormy weather at the top, and many of the hikers were having problems breathing. They could not get them down fast enough and were heading farther down for extra help.

"Take him with you," she said, pointing to Tex.

"I have to rescue Audrey," he gasped.

"You're sick; you need medical attention."

"No. She's my responsibility. I'm not leaving her up there alone." Tex set his jaw.

Deliah waved Prosper on. "She must be pretty special to be worth all this trouble."

The snow swirled around them as the wind picked up. Tex took one last look at the lights twinkling high up the mountain. It would claim whomever it wanted, special or not.

Day 11. 7:00 am, Dar es Salaam, Tanzania

The man with the crooked nose watched through the window of the hotel reception office. Two men in police uniforms forced open the door of the room belonging to the American from Texas. A few minutes later, they emerged with the boy's backpack. The American had eluded them.

㉝ Downhill Slide

Day 11. 11:30 am, Mt. Kilimanjaro, Tanzania

Soft puffs of white cotton swirled gently around her. She dreamed of a fluffy down comforter and sleeping for days. She was falling, dropping gently into a sea of marshmallows.

"Congratulations, Bayer. Didn't think you would make it." Frederick released his grip on her to mark something in a book. He nodded to Freda, "Head down quickly, the weather is turning."

"I made it to the top?" Audrey was in shock. For so long she had just stared at her feet and the rocks beneath them. She had climbed a mountain!

"Come, I know a faster way down." Freda said.

"I thought we went back the Marangu route."

"Trust me. This way is better." Freda was determined, and Audrey didn't want to get separated from her. Plus, she was too tired to argue. The snow began falling faster, making it even more difficult to get a solid footing in the sliding shale. Freda seemed to have fewer problems staying upright.

Audrey could just make out the paths leading in different directions and a sign pointing to the Kibo Huts.

Freda took the trail opposite. Audrey suddenly felt a chill. It wasn't from the snow or the cold. She remembered reading about this trail in her guidebook. It was an up only route. Why was Freda taking her this way?

"Freda? Audrey called out. Freda glanced back. The look in her eyes startled Audrey so much that her feet slipped out beneath her. She fell, sliding another yard on her back, wrenching her knee while trying to avoid a large boulder. The pain mixed with the feeling that something wasn't right.

She reached into the side pocket of her pack and felt for the rope and carbineer. They had used these when they practiced repelling. It was an odd feeling that made her wrap the rope around her waist, before clipping the excess loops to a quick-release snap on her belt.

When she looked up, Freda was gone.

"Allison!"

"Where are you?" Audrey answered.

"Below you." Audrey noticed Freda's voice sounded strained. Did she have a problem?

Audrey rushed toward the sound of Freda's voice, grabbing a rock to lower herself down over a drop-off. She saw the top of Freda's head on the ledge below.

"Help is coming!" Audrey looped the line attached to her belt around a nearby rock and tugged twice to make sure it set.

As Audrey lowered herself to the narrow ledge, she couldn't help but notice the view was amazing. They had dropped below the clouds and she could see swirls of white, shifting to blues, browns, and then greens as the mountain fell into the rain forest.

"Freda?" A chill came over her as hands pushed her. The shove jolted her to react instinctively. She leaned back hard, falling on her back, with her pack digging into one side. Her feet slipped, sending stray shale over the ledge. The rocks thudded and cracked, tumbling down the face of Arrow Glacier.

"You shouldn't have lied to me," Freda whispered as she gave Audrey a second shove toward the edge. "I told Fredrick everything."

Audrey struggled to right herself, but she was like a turtle flat on its back. She grabbed at Freda, whose face was contorted in an ugly, red rage.

"I tried to help you!" Audrey yelled. She felt her pack scoot further away from the safety of the mountain. "I trusted you."

"You won't make that mistake again," Freda sneered. "Operation Eagles Nest changes the world. We're running things now."

Audrey's legs dangled into nothingness, her pack sliding until she felt herself tip. The rock cut into her side. She grabbed at air. The ledge was gone. She was falling.

Day 11. 11:30 am, Undisclosed Location

The Leader sent the message in haste. The American's escape gave the Leader no option. The operation had to be moved forward by 48 hours. But they were ready. POTUS was in the pocket. The backup plan was moving into position. Success was expected. Once the pig president was dead, there would be no stopping the revolution.

Americans in all states would see their strength and join the New Order. The Europeans would follow like sheep.

If that missing American boy was an Intel Center spy, the Leader would handle it, alone, if necessary.

㉞
A Helping Hand

Day 11. 12:00 pm, Mt. Kilimanjaro, Tanzania

Audrey's screams bounced off the volcanic walls, but she sounded near. Tex scrambled across the rocks to the ledge and saw the safety line. He grabbed it just before it slipped off its anchor. He willed his thoughts to focus on Audrey, and not on the pounding in his head and heart.

Deliah fell in behind him, and they leaned back and pulled. Hand over hand, they hauled on the rope.

Fingers from below frantically pawed at the ledge. "I got you, Aud." Tex pulled her toward him. He could feel her head pressed into his chest, her body quaking. "I got you, Aud. I got you, Aud," he kept saying as he stroked her hair. He was hugging a girl, and this time, he wasn't planning on letting go.

"Steady, you two," Deliah said as she helped both of them move away from the edge.

"Who are you?" Audrey asked in between gasps.

"This is Deliah," Tex said. "Or Agent DEAL-MAKER. If it wasn't for her, we would have never found you."

"Thanks," Audrey whispered.

"Good thing you were using your safety line," Tex said, helping Audrey to her feet. "Otherwise, you'd be flat as a fritter." At that moment, Tex's knees gave out. He fought to make it look natural. The wave of nausea hit him again. No way could he throw up in front of Audrey again.

"I was pushed. I didn't fall."

"By who?" Tex asked, willing his stomach to stay put.

Audrey knelt down, so they were face to face. "The agent I recruited." Audrey gave Tex a sheepish smile, which fell away when her warm green eyes met his. "Are you okay?"

"Never been better." Tex held her gaze, wondering, hoping that she would understand what he meant.

"We need to get off this mountain now," Deliah said. "Tex needs to drop below 10,000 feet. Plus, the Dik Diks have a head start, and I have a feeling you're not going to like what Tex and I have learned."

Audrey looped her arm around Tex and together they half slid, half walked down the steep grade as the path opened up. Tex felt giddy and it wasn't the altitude. Audrey was there, next to him. Safe. With the mountain at their back, Tex shared their updates, and Audrey told them what Freda had said about Operation Eagles Nest changing the world.

"We'll need to check in with MOLECHECK, but you shouldn't be seen at the camp," Deliah said. "It's better the Dik Diks believe you're dead."

"The operation takes place in the Rocky Mountains, although I'm not sure where," Audrey added as an afterthought.

"The President's Retreat," Tex said with certainty.

Day 11. 8:00 pm, Dar es Salaam Airport, Tanzania

Frederick hit the encryption command on the laptop. The plain text message turned into a mess of numbers and symbols.

With the American out of the way, he needed new contact instructions for when their private plane touched down in Colorado. Had the Leader forgotten this, or was Frederick still not completely trusted?

35

Stowaways

Day 12. 11:00 pm, Andrews Air Force Base, USA

The message from MOLECHECK was clear.

URGENT. We believe you may be right to suggest a link between the militia activity and the operation in Africa. I fear there is a mole inside the White House. Find the mole. Be very careful.

Finally. Ria and Lee had spent the past two days going back and forth between Intel Center and the White House for meetings and briefings on the plot against the president. At first, the high level staffers questioned their facts and analysis. Even Crenshaw joined the doubters.

But then, just a few hours ago, Crenshaw asked to have a jet fueled. It struck Ria odd that in the dead of night, Crenshaw would decide to go to the Presidential Retreat. After all, he had put Palanski in charge of the president's detail. Was Crenshaw the mole?

There was only one thing for Ria and Lee to do: tail him.

Using a White House car and driver, they arrived at the air base minutes behind Crenshaw. Rather than going to the departure building, the driver pulled to a stop on the tarmac by the airplane. Ria and Lee jumped out.

"Important documents for Special Agent Crenshaw," Ria called as she climbed the metal stairs to the plane's door. Seeing the White House passes, the guard waved them through. The plane was empty, except for the pilot and co-pilot behind a closed door. Ria dropped the folder marked TOP SECRET on one of the front seats. It was filled with magazines lifted from Crenshaw's office.

"Quick, in here," Lee said, pulling her into a storage area and closing the grey folding doors behind them.

"Ouch, you're squishing me," Ria complained.

"Shush," Lee whispered. "The guard might hear us."

After much pushing and grunting, they worked themselves into a seated position, back to back, legs folded up against the opposite walls.

"You're still taking more than half of the room," Ria grumbled, pushing on Lee.

"I'm bigger than you."

"Your problem, not mine," Ria snapped.

"Shush," Lee said. "I hear footsteps."

"Are we ready to go?" It was Crenshaw.

"Yes, sir. The kids gone?" The guard asked.

"Kids?" Crenshaw said.

"Yes, sir, they said they had an important file for you. Left it on your seat." Ria watched Crenshaw reach for the folder through a crack in the door. He shook his head and threw the magazines across the aisle. If he had any suspicions, he didn't have time to act. The plane started its taxi and federal regulations stated that all passengers must be in their seats with their seat belts fastened, even the Special Buffoon-in-Charge.

The wheels hitting the runway woke Ria, and she nudged Lee—or tried to. Her body was numb from being stuck in the same position for four hours.

"I want the plane turned around and ready for take-off in a few hours," Crenshaw said.

"So how do you suggest we get off this thing without anyone noticing?" Ria whispered.

"We follow the pilots off. I'm betting they take a break while the plane is refueled, and we hide in the woods," Lee said. "Let's be ready to run."

Once the cabin and the cockpit were empty, they headed down the aisle to the open door. As Ria's eyes began to adjust to the dark, she could see the lights of the compound in the distance and dark figures that moved in and out of the shadows along the runway. Guards, Ria mouthed to Lee, pointing to the shadows. It figured a Presidential Retreat would be well guarded. No one was going to believe they were here to save the president.

The arrival of Crenshaw gave them a few moments of

distraction, and they bounded down the stairs before diving into the brush on the edge of the runway.

"We better find a good hiding spot, and fast. Maybe someplace warm?" Lee said, steam rising out of each wheezing breath.

"I doubt anyone is going to invite us in for milk and cookies, if that was what you were thinking. There are eyes all around us. We stay put, or we'll walk right into a trap. I'm going to see if we have any messages." Ria pulled her arms out of the sleeves of her jacket and slipped under it like it was the cone of silence. She powered up the secure phone MOLECHECK had issued and hoped the thick jacket would hide the light.

Seconds later, Ria popped out like a jack-in-the-box, startling Lee.

"What?"

"Nothing. Nada. There's no signal up here," Ria said

"Or someone's blocking it."

"Could be the mole, cutting off commo, a chink in the armor that surrounds the president."

"Crenshaw?" Lee said. "Think about it. Don't you think he had to know about the plumbing problem at Camp David?"

"Yeah, but Palanski's equally fishy and what about the lapel pin in the lock?" Ria said.

"That could belong to anyone in the Secret Service."

They were both silent for a moment, watching, listening.

"What do we do if the attack happens today?" Lee asked. "No one knows we're up here. Including MOLECHECK."

"We stop 'em."

"Just you and me. Like how?"

Ria looked out into the darkness. "I have no clue."

Day 13. 1:00 am, Rocky Mountains, Colorado

The planes landed on a private airstrip supplied by a wealthy donor. They were quickly covered with special tarps, white as the surrounding snow. The attack team, also dressed in white, blended into the snowy mountainside. No one had seen anything, and no one knew they were coming.

(36)

War Zone

Day 13. 4:00 am, Presidential Retreat, Colorado

Audrey ducked low and ran. She hoped Tex was right behind her. Now was not the time for Tex to go off on his own. The assault had begun. MOLECHECK had told them the guard house would be a safe place to organize their search for Ria and Lee.

Shadows moved in and out of lights around the perimeter of the president's retreat 500 feet away. There was no way to tell if they were friend or foe. Machine gun fire filled the air. Audrey shuddered. It was like training all over again, except the good guys were shooting back at the Dik Diks. Someone could get hurt, or worse.

Over the edge of the ridge, the shapes appeared to move in

relays before disappearing into the protective cover of the trees. Flashes lit the night sky, followed by a deafening, staccato roar.

Tex slide in next to her once she reached the door.

"Stand back," Tex said. "I'll go in first. Cover me."

The next thing Audrey heard in the darkness was a "Wha…...Ahhhh…!" And then a loud thump. When she leaned in after him, something hard hit her in the head. She stumbled, tripped as something wrapped around her ankles, and hit the ground.

A flashlight switched on.

"Owww. Ria! Put on your sitting britches," Tex said after Ria kicked him again.

"Sweet Einstein, are we glad to see you guys!" Lee said, dropping the clipboard.

"Really?" Audrey said. She rubbed her head where the clipboard had smacked her. "Not the welcome we were expecting. A hello, a cup of tea, that would be a nice—"

"How did you even find us?" Ria interrupted as she coiled up the telephone cord.

"Is that what attacked me?" Audrey said, pointing at the stretchy cord.

Ria rolled her eyes. "No, I did. Aren't you supposed to be in Africa?"

"We were, but MOLECHECK brought us back. And when you didn't respond to MOLECHECK's messages, he tracked you back to a White House driver who said he had dropped two kids with badges off in front of Crenshaw's plane. MOLECHECK agreed to get us up here to keep you guys out of the line of fire. Security is as busy as a hound in flea season right now," Tex said.

"Does no one think Ria and I are capable of completing a mission on our own? We are not just analysts," Lee protested.

"We're just doing our jobs, man," Tex said.

A loud boom shook the guard house. They dove for cover. Ria switched off the flashlight and the four of them huddled on the floor. The wooden floor rattled as the explosions drew closer. The fighting sounded like it was all around them. Would it ever stop? Audrey tried counting to make her mind focus on something other than the storm of emotions churning in and around her.

Audrey counted to sixty fifteen times. Or was it sixteen times? She started over, now counting quiet times, which grew longer and longer. When it had been ages and she lost track again, Audrey wiggled to the wall and pulled herself up to the bottom of the window, using her scarf to clear a small circle in the glass.

American soldiers in winter camouflage uniforms marched their captives across the grounds. The dogs had been let loose, their barking echoing through the woods. They were looking for any strays. Flashlight beams danced upon the trees making the pines seem alive and ready to pounce. Audrey's skin tingled in alarm.

"There's someone out there," Audrey said.

"I don't see anything," Ria said pushing up next to her.

"I feel it," Audrey said. "Shsssh. Everyone down and quiet."

They waited. This time, there was no sound of snow

crunching under boots, but something was definitely moving outside. Slowly, silently.

When the door opened for the second time, Audrey sprang like a cat, catching the intruder by surprise. They rolled, hitting the wall.

Ria switched on her flashlight and shined it on the captive's face.

"You…" the blonde girl stuttered, staring at Audrey.

"Alive, no thanks to you, Freda." Audrey pinned her arms, but struggled to keep the stronger girl down.

Tex grabbed a roll of duct tape from his jacket and with Lee's help, bound the girl's wrists together.

Ria looked from Audrey to Tex. "You know this girl? Who is she?"

Audrey's full attention was channeled on Freda, blocking out everyone else in the hut.

"You weren't successful after all," Audrey said. "Your operation is finished."

"It's just beginning," Freda said with a smirk.

"Guys, time out; don't you think you should bring Lee and me up to speed?" Ria said. "Who is this girl?"

Audrey looked deep into Freda's eyes and sensed she was holding back. What did Freda know? "I saved your life once. You need my help again. We missed something. What don't we know, Freda?"

Freda closed her eyes, shutting Audrey out.

"Lee and I believe there is a mole inside the Secret Service," Ria said. "How else could they have known the president would be here? Can this girl tell us who?"

Freda struggled against Audrey's grip. "Tell me now, or we'll call the soldiers."

"It's gotta be Crenshaw or Palanski," Ria said. "They made the decision to move the president and bring her here."

"Cooperate, Freda. Life in prison is a long time for someone your age." Audrey shook her hard.

"I can't, I won't." Freda hissed eyes again on Audrey. "I don't know anything. I was never told anything."

"You're lying. Your eyes betray you. What did Frederick tell you," Audrey said, her voice just a whisper.

"Who's Frederick?" Ria demanded.

In the silence, an owl hooted and a dog barked. When Freda finally spoke, her words were halted. "The Leader... the American. A plan, a trigger, or signal...must be clear. Your president's assassination. Then the people would know it was time to rise up and bring in the New Order. If our attack failed...then yes, the mole would finish it." Freda turned her head away and closed her eyes.

"Who is the mole?" Audrey demanded.

The next words were a whisper. "The mole is..."

Day 13. 4:30 am, Across America

Freedom Federation leaders mobilized their networks to wait for the signal. Once the president's death was announced, the National Guard units would secure city centers. The Federation would give the orders from then on. A state of emergency would be declared, telling all citizens to stay home. The arrests would begin immediately. True Americans would have a choice: join the Federation or be enemies of the New Order.

37
Mole Bait

Day 13. 6:00 am, Presidential Retreat, Colorado

The White House badges centered on their chests like bullseyes. It took under three minutes from the time Lee and Ria stepped out of the woods before they had a full security escort personally guiding them towards the Secret Service operations center. It was exactly where they wanted to be.

Lee heard Crenshaw bellowing before the door even opened. Inside, monitors mounted on the wall glowed in eerie green, showing the grounds and mop-up operation still ongoing. In the center of the spacious room, bathed in the green glow, Palanski and nine other Secret Service agents stood at attention.

Crenshaw was demanding to know who had authorized

the military strike, since last time he looked that was his job. And if the Secret Service's finest were cowering in this room, WHO, he wanted to know, was watching the president?

"What the—!" were the next words uttered as Crenshaw turned toward Lee, his face a mixture of anger and confusion. Palanski turned and glared at them, too.

"Sir, I will check on the president this instant. And I am sorry for the unexpected incident. I had no idea, either." Palanski stepped toward the door when Crenshaw hollered again. "You will go nowhere until I get the full story!"

Lee moved into the room. "Special Agent in Charge Crenshaw, the plot launched by the European branch of the Freedom Federation has failed." Lee intended to sound in control, but his voice cracked and squeaked at the end of 'failed.' "We have captured an enemy agent who has confessed."

"What?" Crenshaw said, looking at Lee like he was some alternative form of life.

All the agents had turned and were staring at Lee now. His insides felt squishy. Why did he ever think Crenshaw would listen?

Suddenly, Ria was at his side and pointing directly at Palanski. "You were the one who said Camp David was under construction and recommended moving the president here. Convenient change of plans or master plan?" All eyes turned from Ria to Agent Palanski.

"I think the bigger question would be what are you two even doing here?" Palanski snarled back.

"We're here to catch a mole," Ria said.

"What are you talking about?" Crenshaw demanded. He signaled at their armed escort to remove them from the ops center.

"And to stop the blackmailing of Todd Geringer and the vice president," Lee added, not budging when the escort moved to flank him and Ria.

"Somebody's blackmailing the vice president?" Crenshaw said, running his hands over the bristles of his chin. He was listening now.

Sweet Einstein. Lee knew his moment had come. He pulled out his pen and held it high. His invention would save the day. He wished Tex was there to witness that Lee was more than a paper pusher, but a real spy armed with science. He pressed on the pen top with his thumb and waited.

Nothing happened.

"This is ridiculous," Palanski said, heading toward the door.

Lee clicked the pen again, then again. Nothing.

Panicking, Lee smacked the pen against the helmet of the closest escort.

Palanski stopped dead in his tracks as a voice filled the room.

They have a mole in the Secret Service. How else could they have known the president would be here? Can this girl tell us who? It was Ria's voice. *It's either Crenshaw or Palanski. They made the decision for the president to come here.*

Palanski remained motionless.

Audrey's voice rang clear and strong from the pen.

Cooperate, Freda. Life in prison is long for someone your age.

A female's voice with a heavy German accent said, *I can't, I won't. I don't know anything. I was never told anything.*

Palanski started and then recovered, but not fast enough to escape Lee's trained observation skills.

You're lying. Your eyes betray you. What did Frederick tell you? The Leader...the American. A plan, a trigger, or signal...must be clear. Your president's assassination. Then the people would know it was time to rise up and bring in the New Order. If our attack failed...then yes, the mole would finish it."

Who is the mole, Freda?

The mole is—

Lee hit the off switch and chaos broke out.

Palanski reached inside his jacket.

"He's gotta gun!" screamed Lee, pointing at Palanski before knocking Ria out of the way of danger.

A pile of Secret Service agents landed on Palanski, taking him to the ground. It looked like a giant octopus, with the multiple arms and legs moving independently. The thrashing slowed to a stop. The Secret Service agents stood, all except Palanski. He was in handcuffs, his gun on the floor. A stream of foul words colored his otherwise pale face.

"When did you figure out it was Palanski?" Ria asked Lee as the room began to clear. "If Freda didn't know, how could you? And how'd you know he'd pull a gun? They all have guns."

Lee grinned. "Yes, but only the mole would want to use it."

㉛ Puzzle Solved

Day 13. 7:00 am, Presidential Retreat, Colorado

Ria marched on the heels of the Secret Service escort, with Tex, Lee, and Audrey following behind her, down the spiral metal staircase into the depths of the mountain. The president and her family had been evacuated and were safely back at the White House. The Junior Spies stood inside the Situation Room. It was the command center from which presidents handled crises, led wars, and authorized the use of nuclear weapons. Ria felt right at home.

An oversized monitor, surrounded by eight smaller screens, covered one wall. Seated at the table was MOLECHECK, eyes twinkling.

"Is this thing on?" CONTROL demanded as her face

moved in on the camera, growing bigger and bigger until her nose covered the entire screen. Imposing in real life, the three-foot-wide image of CONTROL's nostrils was downright scary.

Satisfied, CONTROL finally stepped back, restoring the picture, and her control, over the debriefing. The sound was perfectly clear, offering no clue that the digital bits had each been encoded, scrambled, transmitted by burst technology 10,000 miles to a spy satellite, relayed, unscrambled, and decoded before being projected again.

"You've received our report from the African operation?" MOLECHECK said.

"Yes, and I have just spoken to the directors of the Secret Service and FBI about Palanski and the militia. They have arrested the leader here in the U.S. There are a few loose ends we still need to tie up from the foreign ops side." CONTROL held up a picture of a man in handcuffs, standing between two uniformed police officers. "MIND-READER, is this the man you saw at the Dik Dik camp?"

"Yes," Audrey said, eyes growing wide. "That's Frederick!"

"So if Plan A—the Dik Dik assault team—failed, Palanski was Plan B because he was trusted and could get next to Mrs. P.," Ria jumped in.

"What I still don't understand," Lee interrupted, "is why they planned such a complicated assault when Palanski could have killed the president at any time."

Audrey chimed in. "Freda said they wanted a defining moment to encourage supporters to rise up en masse and change the government, first in the U.S. and then in Europe.

Their first act of business was deporting all immigrants."

"What about Todd and the Vice President?" Lee asked.

"What about the surveillance team at the Kili Cafe?" Tex said at the same time.

CONTROL held up her hand to silence them. "I'm asking the questions." She looked down at something off screen. "Palanski was blackmailing Todd we believe in order to control him once the vice president became president." She held up a second photo. The camera zoomed in, showing a blonde teen. "COW-BOY and MIND-READER, do you recognized this girl?"

"Yeah, she was in the café, obviously sent to smoke us out," Tex said. "What about the man with the crooked nose? DEAL-MAKER said I was seeing ghosts, but I know surveillance when I see it. He followed us from Dar es Salaam to Moshi. You can bet the farm on it."

MOLECHECK cleared his throat. "No, COW-BOY, you weren't seeing ghosts."

When MOLECHECK didn't go on, Tex pressed. "Give me the bacon without the sizzle."

"CONTROL?" MOLECHECK asked with deference.

CONTROL's lips pursed to the point they almost disappeared. Finally, she said, "He was part of the backup team, responsible for exfiltration – getting you out – if the op went sideways."

"What?" Tex's temper flashed, but Ria had no intention of letting him ruin the finale of her first ops success.

"Sizzle down your ego, COW-BOY," Ria warned.

"Now, where was I," CONTROL said, running her fingers through her short brown hair. "The police have arrested millionaire Barry VanderCourt and judging by the money trail, we believe he is the Leader. So far, he is denying he was in charge. A review of his bank accounts shows a number of large money transfers to a bank in Liechtenstein and large payments to a Russian gunrunner, General Stone of the US National Guard, Capitol Police Chief Griffin, and the media giant Roger Steiner."

CONTROL was momentarily distracted as a note was slipped into her hand. "In any case, if we can trace the money, we can make sure Barry VanderCourt and the others go to prison for a very long time."

CONTROL's face suddenly contorted. Ria wasn't sure if it was a facial spasm or a smile. "I will see you all back in Washington. You performed well on your first mission and for that we are proud of you."

There was a moment of static and then the screen went dark.

39

Shattered Pictures

Day 15. 3:00 pm, White House, Washington D.C.

"Sweet Einstein," Lee said to himself. He and Tex were in the Oval Office for a photo op with the president. Tex looked lost and a bit confused, touching everything like he was checking to see if it was real. Tex had been unusually quiet ever since he came back from Africa. Lee didn't know why. Tex and Audrey had had the adventure of a lifetime. As the camera crew set up, CONTROL and MOLECHECK chatted with the new head of the Secret Service. Today was a day for celebration. After the photo op, they would all be sent home and life would be, well, back to normal.

Ria and Audrey burst into the room in giggles. Ria was holding several files.

"Come with me to turn in our final reports," Ria said nudging Lee. "It's our last time in Crenshaw's office. It sort of feels like we should do it together, even though he's not there."

"The president arrives in fifteen minutes." MOLECHECK tapped his watch.

"Back in a flash," Ria hollered as they headed down the hall.

"I can't believe that after today we'll never walk these halls again. I'm going to miss this place," Lee said.

"I thought you hated being trapped in our smelly dungeon."

"Yeah, but you gotta admit, we were close to the action. Our little bit of history."

"I'm just hoping to get out of here without having to give this up." Ria held up her precious badge with the large red 'A'.

"Good luck with that," Lee laughed. "I'll be sure to stand out of the way when Security tackles you at the door."

"I can give them a run for their money."

"I have no doubt."

The scent of patchouli and vanilla filled the hall before Lee saw her. "Hi, Mrs. Werner," Lee said. Mrs. Werner was heading down the hall with a tray filled with cups and a pot of tea.

"You're headed the wrong way, sweetie," Mrs. Werner said as she adjusted her tray.

"Just dropping off our final report," Lee said. "Can we help you?"

"NO, no thank you." Mrs. Werner suddenly seemed distracted as she pushed past them. Maybe she was still upset about Crenshaw and Palanski.

"Does everyone seem a little jumpy to you?" Lee said when Mrs. Werner was safely out of earshot.

"I think they're all just tired. Maybe tired of us."

Ria placed the folder on Mrs. Werner's desk and pulled a note out of her pocket, placing it on top.

"What's that?" Lee grabbed for the note.

"It's a thank you note from both of us. I used one of Mrs. Edencamp's notecards."

"Then I want to see it."

"You'll just mess everything up."

"I'm just reading," Lee said. "Not messing." He reached for the note, but Ria promptly snatched it out of his hand. He reached back around her as she started to twist away from him.

"Give," he said as he tried to worm his way around her. Ria twisted around again. Lee fell against the desk. The two picture frames Mrs. Werner kept near her computer went flying.

"Quick, pick 'em up," Ria said falling to her knees. Lee stepped towards her and heard a dull crunch against the thick carpet.

"Oops."

Ria picked up the frame, the glass was cracked in all directions, and there was a deep gouge in the middle.

"Look what you did, you big oaf."

Lee took the picture from her and leaned it against the desk lamp. It was of Mrs. Werner and another woman.

"The woman with Mrs. Werner looks really familiar," Ria said.

"They both look a lot alike," Lee said. "They both have poodle hair and diamond dog collars."

"That's it!" Ria gasped.

"What?"

"They're sisters."

"Who?"

"Mrs. Werner and this woman. They're sisters."

"So?"

"So, this is Barry VanderCourt's wife!"

They both just stared at each other for a moment. The president was scheduled to arrive at the Oval Office any moment now. There was no Secret Service assigned inside the room, save the new head of detail. Everyone, including CONTROL and MOLECHECK thought those behind the assassination attempt had been stopped and arrested.

Lee looked at Mrs. Werner's desk, full of two sets of items. "A double agent," Lee said after a moment.

"A what?"

"Plan A was stopped, and we exposed Plan B. Nobody thought about Plan C. Mrs. Werner is Plan C."

"How do we warn CONTROL?"

"We don't have time, Ria. We have to fix this ourselves. Isn't it kind of odd that Mrs. Werner was included today and in charge of the tea?"

"So she's going to spill hot tea on the president?" Ria asked.

"No. It's gotta be something much worse."

㊿ Plan C

Day 15. 3:15 pm, White House, Washington D.C.

"You protect the president while I take down Mrs. Werner," Lee said, wheezing as they rushed down the hall.

"Absolutely," Ria said as they burst through the door to the Oval Office.

Lee scanned the room from left to right, remembering his spy school training. POTUS sat at the massive desk centered between the windows. Standing to her left were Audrey and Tex. CONTROL, MOLECHECK, and the new head of the Secret Service stood at the back of the room, near the door.

Mrs. Werner was just setting the tea tray on the coffee table. "I guess this is my signal to leave," she said. "I see you all have a photo shoot."

She started toward Lee and then made an abrupt turn toward the president.

"Poodle!" Lee shouted as he sprang into action.

Ria sprinted across the room and leapt for the president's desk, landing on her belly, arms outstretched as she slid across its well-polished surface. The president caught Ria, the force knocking both of them to the floor.

A look of horror came over CONTROL and MOLECHECK as the head of the Secret Service reached for his gun. Lee didn't have time to explain.

"I'M SOOO SORRRRRRRYYYYYYY, MRS. WERNER!" Lee lowered his head and ran at her like a human battering ram. His head found his target, the soft middle of her stomach. The air went out of her like a popped balloon as she folded.

"Lee!" CONTROL's voice could be heard above the commotion. Then there was a collective gasp as Mrs. Werner struggled to a sitting position with a grenade in her right hand. With her left, she reached up and pulled the safety pin.

Tex dove at her, wrapping his hands around Mrs. Werner's, keeping the hand grenade lever locked down. Mrs. Werner struggled against Tex, trying to break the grenade free.

"Grab the pin," Tex yelled.

Lee tried to sit up, but a shooting pain down his neck and left side of his torso stopped him.

Mrs. Werner threw the pin into the air and, with her newly free hand, fought even harder against Tex's hold.

"FIND THE PIN!" Audrey yelled. "HICHORY DICKORY DOCK." Audrey flew with the lightness of a ballerina over Tex to Lee. Her hands searched the dark carpet. "THE MOUSE RAN UP THE CLOCK."

Lee rolled onto his belly to search around him. "Found it," he yelled, the small metal wire digging into his stomach. He tossed it to Audrey. While she was a graceful dancer, she was not a natural at the game of catch. The pin flew just past her head and bounced off the president's desk.

"THE CLOCK STRUCK TEN," Audrey yelled, hopping backwards, following the pin to the floor next to the desk.

Audrey grabbed the pin once again. "AND DOWN HE RAN."

Tex wrenched the hand grenade free of Mrs. Werner's grasp and with the lever still pressed down, vaulted toward Audrey. At the same time, Lee rolled, pinning Mrs. Werner to the floor with his bulk.

"HICHORY DICKORY…" Audrey pushed the safety pin into the grenade in Tex's outstretched hand and yelled "DOCK" as the circuit broke and the grenade was rendered safe once again.

In the ten seconds it took Audrey to secure the grenade, the new head of the Secret Service had Mrs. Werner cuffed, and the room filled with security and a bomb squad to dispose of the grenade.

"Th-thannnnk you," the president stammered as Ria and Audrey helped her to her feet and brushed stray carpet lint from her suit before she was whisked away by her security detail.

Lee remained where he was on the floor. He was still

stunned and dizzy. Audrey came over to help him, but he stopped her when pain shot through him. "I'm good, Aud. But what's with the nursery rhymes?"

"Yeah," Ria pipped up. "Can this get any weirder?"

"That's how I learned to keep the timing straight. You know, it takes ten seconds and that's all you have."

"Yeah, once the lever has been released. Hey, whatever," Tex said, grinning at Audrey.

"Can someone explain what is going on here?" CONTROL demanded.

"Everyone thought the president was safe after stopping Plans A and B, but no one considered there could be a Plan C," Ria said. "Tell 'em Lee."

Through gritted teeth, Lee explained. "Ria and I put it all together when we saw the picture on Mrs. Werner's desk of Mrs. Werner with another women. They looked so much alike, they had to be sisters. Then Ria remembered seeing this other woman in an article when we were doing research on Mr. VanderCourt. Turns out, she is Mrs. VanderCourt."

Pausing to catch his breath, Lee continued. "It all made sense. Ria and I saw Mrs. Warner and Palanski at a dead drop in the Mall. Plus, she brought Swiss chocolates back from a European vacation at the same time the Leader was in Liechtenstein, and she knew everything that was happening with the president's security detail."

CONTROL looked over at MOLECHECK, and Lee could have sworn he saw a slight smile.

The team got their photo with the president that day.

After endless debriefings, congratulations, plus a trip to the Emergency Room to check out his head and neck, Lee drifted off to sleep that night with the photo propped on his nightstand and dreamed of how he helped save the day.

㊶ Among Friends

Day 16. 8:00 pm, Intel Center, Dulles, Virginia

Lee hurried along the walkway between the planes trying to catch Tex but careful not to move his arm, now in a sling.

"Hey wait up," Lee shouted. Tex finally stopped. Lee gave him a friendly punch in the shoulder. "What are you doing?"

"I never had a chance to look around the Air and Space Museum," Tex said. "MOLECHECK said it was best at night, when everyone was gone. He was right. You can actually climb into some of the cockpits."

They had returned to Intel Center for their final debriefing. Waiting for them were endless piles of paperwork, all needing to be completed before they could return home. Lee planned on catching a train to New York the first thing in the morning.

After dislocating his shoulder during his tackle of Mrs. Werner, his mother had pushed to have him sent home earlier. He didn't know what Tex's plans were.

"I'm happy experiencing the planes from the ground," Lee said.

"Yeah, but you can see everything from the cockpit."

"Will I be able to see what's bugging you?" Lee asked.

"What makes you think something's bothering me?" Tex said, avoiding eye contact with Lee.

"Well, you might be able to fool Ria, but you can't fool me or Audrey. Something's wrong. I thought maybe I could help."

"It's nothing," Tex said, his voice thick.

"Try me, or I'll sic Audrey on you."

Tex forced a laugh.

Lee waited, but Tex was studying his boots. "You know by now you can trust me."

"Have you ever felt like you just don't do anything right?"

Lee started laughing. "Only every day."

"I messed up so many times on this mission. Audrey almost died because of me. I wouldn't be surprised if she never trusted me again."

"Well, Audrey didn't die, and why are you so worried about what she'd think anyway?"

"Because…" Tex said, eyes on the floor, "never mind, it doesn't matter."

"Hellloooo?" A singsong sound voice rang out. It was Audrey, being Audrey.

"We're over here," Lee called out. Moments later, Audrey

skipped around an airplane with Ria.

"Wow," Lee said. "You got your hair back." Audrey's red locks were hanging in pretty waves at her shoulders.

"VIOLET used a color stripper. So I'm me again."

"You guys planning on hijacking one of these planes?" Ria asked.

Tex forced a grin. "That's an idea. I could fly it to my next mission."

"You have a new assignment!?" Lee asked. "When were you going to tell us?"

"He's yanking your chain," Ria said.

"Actually, I'm not. But it's Audrey's fault."

Audrey gasped. "My fault? What did I do?"

"Your mom told CONTROL that I was having trouble at school."

"I'm sure my mom was just trying to help. Please don't be mad," Audrey pleaded.

"I'm not; in fact I'm grateful. CONTROL is sending me to a boarding school somewhere in Europe. There's a boy there who likes to race. His father runs the biggest illegal drug network in Europe. CONTROL thinks I can become this kid's new best friend."

"What about the rest of us?" Ria demanded. "It's not like we all didn't work together on this operation."

Lee laughed. "Ria, I'm sure CONTROL has something in her petri dish for all of us."

"Can we just enjoy these last few moments together?" Audrey said.

"Okay," Ria squeezed Lee tight, then yelped. "That dumb pen of yours is sharp."

"Oh, I almost forgot." Lee took the pen from his pocket and clicked it three times. Music began playing as photos flashed on the walls and the sides of the planes. There was Ria, head down on her desk sleeping, with a crushed bagel stuck to her curls. Audrey twirling in the Oval Office, skirt flying high. Tex making faces in the Situation Room when CONTROL couldn't see him, and about a dozen more embarrassing shots of Crenshaw, Palanski, Marshall, and Todd.

"Where did you get these?" Ria screeched.

"MOLECHECK gave me a tie clip camera. I figured if those guys didn't confess, I could send the pics to an online gossip blog."

"Or just stick them in a small room with Ria," Tex said.

"You're lucky you're leaving the country."

"Group hug," Audrey said.

Lee wrapped his good arm around Ria, as Tex wrapped an arm around his neck and Audrey carefully avoided his shoulder and squeezed his hand. Operation Kili may have tested them in different ways, but once again, they had come through as a team and as friends. They were the best friends Lee had ever had.

Day 16. 3:00 am, Netherlands

The car sped through the countryside, the headlights on low. It was a custom racecar, built from scratch with fake panels packed with $2.5 million in drugs. The car handled like it was on rails. Until right before the tire blew.

Poem Codes

Poem codes are a form of substitution ciphers. The key for encrypting and decrypting is drawn from a poem or set phrase. The Freedom Federation 'poem' was "True Americans Must Stand Together to Purify and Save the Nation."

When Ria and Lee suspected that the Jumble was an encrypted message, Ria looked at the first 5-letter group (ACGIJ) for the clue on how to begin breaking the coded message. A is the first letter of the alphabet and therefore she selected the first word of the poem: True. C is the third letter, so Ria used the third word of the poem: Must. The key for this message is:

T R U E M U S T P U R I F Y S A V E T H E.

The next step is to substitute numbers for letters. The first A is assigned 1 (in the word SAVE). Number 2 is assigned to the next A (there is none in this case) or the next letter in the alphabet (there is no B, C, or D). Therefore, the E in "TRUE" is assigned 2. The E in "SAVE" is assigned 3. The E in "THE" is assigned 4 and so on.

It is easiest to do the work on a piece of grid paper. The code key now looks like this:

T=14	M=8	P=9	S=13	T=16
R=10	U=18	U=19	A=1	H=6
U=17	S=12	R=11	V=20	E=4
	E=2	T=15	I=7	E=3

F=5

Y=21

On the grid paper, write the numbers in order across the page:

14 10 17 2 8 18 12 15 9 19 11 7 5 21 13 1 20 3 16 6 4

Step three uses the code key and the 5-letter groupings of the Jumble.

ACGIJ AOJSK FORMO CXSID NSNIM
HTPKA JEGTO SLGSH CSFAA VQNNI
PBWOU PTDYI QLAGB UEZRS

On the grid paper, number across the page, starting at 1 and ending at 21. Ria will start with number 14 from the code key and the second group of the 5 letters from the Jumble. (The first group has already been used to identify which words from the poem to use): AOJSK. The first 3 letters of the 5-letter group will be assigned to the number 14.

1 2 3 4 5 6 7 8 9 10 11 12 13 14 15 16 17 18 19 20 21

A

O

J

Using the remaining 2 letters from the same 5-letter group (SK) and the first letter from the next 5-letter group, assign these to number 10 (the next number of the code key).

1 2 3 4 5 6 7 8 9 10 11 12 13 14 15 16 17 18 19 20 21

S	A
K	O
F	J

Ria then continues with code key 17, working through all of the code key numbers and the 5-letter groups. Once completed, the grid should look like this (except across the page):

1	2	3	4	5	6	7	8	9	10	11	12	13	14	15
P	O	T	U	S	A	S	S	A	S	I	N	A	T	
B	C	D	E	F	G	H	I	J	K	L	M	N	O	P
W	X	Y	Z	A	B	C	D	E	F	G	H	I	J	K

16	17	18	19	20	21
I	O	N	G	O	A
Q	R	S	T	U	V
L	M	N	O	P	Q

The decrypted message is on the first line. If the message had been longer, it would have flowed to the second and third line. Once the message is complete, the letters are just gibberish.

POTUS Assassination Go

To encrypt a message using the same code, you reverse the order slightly. You pick the five words you want to use from the poem and you substitute the letters for numbers as in step 2 above. Using the total number count from the poem letters, you then write out your message, with the first line having the same number of letters as your poem letter count and then filling in the remaining letter spots after the message with random letters from the alphabet. Then you go back to your poem word's letters, which have now been substituted with numbers and you start building the 5-letter groups. Your message is now encrypted into a series of 5-letter groups.

About the Authors

Melissa Mahle is a former spy, movie consultant, and nonfiction author.

Kathryn Dennis is a writer and illustrator with a background in marketing and advertising.

Together, Melissa and Kathryn write adventure and espionage stories for middle-grade readers, including the Anatolia Steppe series and the Junior Spy series.

When not writing, Melissa and Kathryn crave adventure and travel to strange places, which takes courage, curiosity of the unknown, and a very strong intestinal tract.

Discover more at www.spygirlspress.com

More from SpyGirls Press

Camp Secret – Junior Spies No. 1
Camp Secret is one fun read! - Chris Grabenstein

Lost in Petra [An Anatolia Steppe Mystery] No.1
Publishers Weekly Starred Review

Uncovered in Istanbul [An Anatolia Steppe Mystery] No. 2

Made in the USA
Middletown, DE
06 October 2016